New Beginnings

clearwater crossing

New Beginnings

laura peyton roberts

BANTAM BOOKS
NEW YORK • TORONTO • LONDON • SYDNEY • AUCKLAND

RL 5.8, age 12 and up
NEW BEGINNINGS
A Bantam Book / February 1999

ISBN 0-553-49256-X

Published simultaneously in the United States and Canada.

Bantam Books are published by Bantam Books, a division of Random
House, Inc. Its trademark, consisting of the words "Bantam Books" and
the portrayal of a rooster, is Registered in U.S. Patent and Trademark
Office and in other countries. Marca Registrada. Bantam Books, 1540
Broadway, New York, New York 10036.

PRINTED IN THE UNITED STATES OF AMERICA

OPM   10   9   8   7   6   5   4   3   2

For Wendy,
who spotted a Ghost in the slush
and gave me a New Beginning.
Thanks.

Your beginnings will seem humble, so prosperous will your future be.

Job 8:7

One

"It's your house," Peter Altmann told Nicole, walking up beside her. "You should do the honors."

Nicole Brewster gazed around her basement rec room at the other laughing, talking members of Eight Prime, an excited smile lighting her face. She had been so sure the group was going to break up after it achieved its goal of buying a bus for the Junior Explorers, but in the end they couldn't bring themselves to call it quits. They bought the bus, then made a new pact—to stay together.

Who'd have guessed? she thought, shaking her head. All eight of them were there that Thursday night, attending their first meeting since the Saturday picnic where they'd agreed to a new beginning. Ben Pipkin and Jesse Jones were filling up on crackers and cheese, Melanie Andrews was sipping bottled water and talking to Leah Rosenthal, Jenna Conrad and Miguel del Rios were enjoying the fancy bakery cookies Mrs. Brewster had brought home, and Peter was at Nicole's side, urging her to call the meeting to order.

Nicole cleared her throat self-consciously. "Does everyone want to sit down?" she called over the chatter. "We'd better get started."

People began drifting from the snack table in back toward the furniture near the center of the room.

"Take those with you," Nicole added, gesturing for Miguel to move the cookie plate to the coffee table.

The group found seats and waited, looking at each other expectantly. No one knew what to say.

"This is weird," Melanie offered after a moment, tucking a strand of her perfect blond hair behind one ear. "It feels strange having a meeting after we already bought the bus and everything. I mean, I'm glad . . . but I never thought I'd be sitting here again. No offense, Nicole."

Nicole nodded, understanding exactly. She hadn't expected to be hanging out at Melanie's house either. Until recently, the two of them had barely spoken to each other.

"It is a little weird," Jenna agreed. "But weird in a good way, right?"

Heads nodded around the room. Even Nicole, who had once been so eager for the group to disband, had to admit she was happy they'd stayed together after all—and she'd leapt at the honor of holding the first new meeting at her house.

"Look," Jenna said, holding up the steno pad she always wrote meeting notes in. "I started a new section for our minutes." A fresh page had been decorated with pink and purple markers: DECEMBER 10, EIGHT PRIME'S NEW BEGINNING.

"We're just full of new beginnings," Leah said, reminding them all that they had originally seen the formation of Eight Prime as a way of starting over after Kurt Englbehrt's death.

"*Life* is full of new beginnings," Jenna replied sincerely.

"All right," Jesse broke in, running an impatient hand over the buzz cut he'd gotten the day before. "Enough with the new beginnings, already. Can we get down to business now?"

"Okay," Peter said. "The first item of business is having Kurt's name painted on the bus."

Ben's hand shot into the air. "I had a dream about this! On the front of the bus, really big, we should paint 'Kurt'; then across the back, 'Englbehrt.' That way people will see his name coming and going."

"Gee, that sounds classy," Nicole said sarcastically. She didn't *like* to put Ben down, but most of his ideas were so dumb. Somebody had to tell him.

"I'm not sure we'll be able to paint anything on the front," Peter said. "There's the grill, and the headlights . . . The back is a better idea. We could paint Kurt's full name there, and maybe even add something—like 'Dedicated to the Children of Clearwater Crossing in Memory of Kurt Englbehrt.' "

3

Leah chuckled. "Good idea. That way when cars get stuck behind it, maybe they won't get as mad."

"I thought we were going to put the writing along both sides," Melanie protested.

"Or maybe we should do something with football," said Miguel. "Like add his jersey number or something."

"That's a good idea!" Jesse cried enthusiastically. Then the discussion broke down completely as everyone started talking at once.

"I have a suggestion," Jenna finally interrupted. "Why doesn't everyone draw up their version of what they think we should do? Then we can look at all the drawings and vote on them later."

"Good idea," said Peter. "We can't get it painted until afterward anyway." He and Jenna exchanged smiles.

"After what?" asked Nicole, curious.

Jenna turned to face her, her steno pad dropping forgotten to her lap. "Peter and I dreamt up the best present ever to give the Junior Explorers this year. We're having a winter camp!"

"Winter camp?" Nicole repeated.

"During the first week of the break from school. The park service at Rabbit Ridge donated two cabins, and we're taking ten kids to the woods for four days. We're leaving on the twenty-first and coming back Christmas Eve."

"Why didn't you tell us before?" Ben demanded

in an injured tone. "I could have been helping you plan!"

Jenna looked surprised.

"Sorry, Ben," Peter said quickly. "For one thing, we just found out ourselves. Besides, this isn't really an Eight Prime event—it's just something Chris and I are doing with the Junior Explorers. Jenna and Maura are coming to help with the girls, and my parents will be there to chaperone, but that's really all we have room for. We'll be packed in like sardines as it is."

"Sounds fun," Nicole fibbed, vastly relieved that no one expected—or even wanted—her to help. The last thing she felt like doing on her precious, hard-earned vacation was working another charity event. No way! Once she got through the next week of exams at school, all she wanted to do was sleep in every morning for two solid weeks. When she rolled out of bed around noon, maybe she'd catch up on her growing stack of magazines. Or, if she was really in the mood to exert herself, she might go to the mall with Courtney and scope out the clothes she planned to buy at the after-Christmas sales. "You'll have to tell us all about it when you get back," she added smugly.

"Is Amy going?" Melanie asked.

Peter nodded. "I think so."

"Isn't it going to be snowing or something?" Jesse asked. "It's so dang cold already, I'm surprised the whole state doesn't migrate south with the birds." As a reluctantly transplanted Californian, Jesse was always complaining about Missouri weather—too hot, too cold, too wet, too whatever. Too far east was what he really meant, and they had all learned to ignore him.

"We hope so," Peter said. "That's the whole point. Chris and I have a couple of old sleds, and we're going to take the kids sledding and show them how to make snowmen and stuff."

"Yeah, right. You mean how to have snowball fights," Miguel corrected, his brown eyes full of longing. "I used to love having snowball fights with my dad."

"Oh, and making snow angels in soft powder. With hot chocolate afterward." Melanie turned to Jenna. "You guys will have so much fun."

"I want to go," Ben whined. "Come on, Peter. I could be a big help!" He stared at Peter with pleading eyes, his hands clasped in front of him imploringly. "Please?"

Peter glanced uncomfortably around the room. "It's not that I don't want to take you, Ben. But if I invite you I have to ask everyone, and we just can't squeeze—"

"You don't have to invite *me*," Nicole hurried to interrupt. "I mean, uh, not with you so short on space and all."

"I won't be offended either," Leah said. "I have a ton of things to do."

Miguel put his hand over hers on the sofa. "My mom'll have a bunch of Christmas stuff planned. I should stay to drive her around."

"See?" Ben said.

Peter glanced at Melanie, then Jesse.

"Don't look at me," Jesse muttered. "I'll still be in yard work hell with my good buddy Charlie."

Melanie shook her head, as if to say she had things planned too.

"Well," Peter said slowly, "I guess if no one else really *wants* to go . . ."

"Yes!" Ben cried triumphantly. "You won't be sorry. When this camp is over, you're going to look back and you won't even be able to imagine it without me there."

That last part's probably true anyway, Nicole thought, trying to keep from smiling. Four days in a cabin with Ben was almost certain to be memorable in one way or another.

"Okay, that's settled," Jenna said, with obvious relief. "So everyone is going to draw up their bus-painting ideas for a later meeting too?"

People nodded, and Jenna made a note.

"How are you paying for camp?" Leah asked Peter. "I mean, gas and food and everything?"

"We're getting the cabins for free, and the kids

7

will be assigned different groceries to bring, like potluck. After that there's only gas and a few incidentals. Jenna and I will pay for those ourselves."

"Don't be silly," Melanie said. "Take the money out of the bus fund. We'll earn it back after the holidays."

"No. You don't have. . . ," Peter began, but the rest of the group backed Melanie up. Peter nodded his thanks, turning a little red as he did.

"Is that all the business?" Jesse asked, pausing to see if anyone spoke up. "Then how about getting together in the park this Saturday for a game of touch football? After Junior Explorers," he added for Peter's benefit. "I'm going to need a break from Charlie's yard."

"That sounds good to me," said Miguel, leaning forward.

"I'm up for it," Leah said.

Jesse stared at her, then shrugged. "Okay, why not? Girls too."

"You weren't even inviting us?" Melanie cried, outraged. "Jesse Jones, you—"

"I said girls too. Geez! And bring friends, everyone. Eight people isn't enough for any kind of game."

"I'm bringing some *girl*friends," Melanie told him pointedly.

"Knock yourself out. Bring the whole cheerleading squad, for all I care."

Nicole's gaze bounced back and forth from Jesse to Melanie, and she wondered how she had ever believed in a romance between them. All that pair ever did was argue.

"Bring Angela!" Ben suggested, naming one of the junior cheerleaders who had helped Eight Prime with its October pumpkin sale. "She's nice."

"I'll see if she wants to come," Melanie replied noncommittally, still glaring at Jesse.

"Okay, I guess that's it, then," Peter said. "What do you all think about waiting until after Christmas to have another meeting? Everyone's going to be busy, and there's really nothing pressing."

"Sounds good to me," Nicole said happily, mentally chalking up some more relaxation time.

The rest of the group agreed, and people started walking toward the stairs.

"Don't forget to work on your bus ideas!" Jenna reminded them, making a final rushed note on her pad.

A minute later they were gone, and Nicole stood looking around the abandoned rec room. Unlike the first time she'd hosted the meeting, when she'd put out a big, splashy spread designed to impress, this time she had limited herself to cookies, crackers with cheese, and a single, medium-sized cooler of drinks. *There are some benefits to not chasing Jesse anymore*, she thought, surveying the five-minute job in front of her and remembering what a nightmare cleanup had been last time.

Then, unbidden, another image from the previous meeting popped into her head: herself hunched over the toilet, forcing a finger down her throat until she vomited. She'd gotten up off the bathroom floor that night so repulsed by her own actions that she'd promised herself she'd never do it again. But she had—after the homecoming game, when Jesse had unexpectedly shown up at the bonfire with Vanessa Winters, the stuck-up cheerleading captain.

Thinking about it now, Nicole wasn't even sure what had driven her to such desperate measures. Both times she had overeaten, and both times she'd been terrified of gaining weight, but somehow she'd convinced herself she was really doing it for Jesse. The weird thing was, though, even now that Jesse had convinced her they'd never be a couple, she still couldn't bear to gain an ounce. Not even his saying she was too skinny had swayed her in the slightest.

Losing weight wasn't about Jesse anymore.

Nicole sighed. She wasn't sure *what* it was about.

"You're quiet tonight," Jesse said from the driver's seat.

Melanie shrugged. She didn't feel like talking.

On the other hand, since he was driving her home, she supposed she ought to make some effort to be pleasant. She couldn't tell him what was really bothering her, of course—if she admitted she was dreading the two weeks off from school she'd sound totally pathetic—but she supposed she could make something up.

"I'm tired, I guess," she mumbled, hoping he'd let it go.

Amazingly, he did. Melanie gradually relaxed into the silence, staring through his dark windshield and letting her mind wander.

By now she knew better than to tell people she hated Christmas. No one ever believed her. Either they didn't want to believe she was the kind of person who could genuinely hate the holiday, or they just couldn't accept that anyone did.

Melanie sighed and sank deeper into Jesse's black leather seat. She didn't know how she was going to face another Christmas as depressing as the last one, the second without her mother. Her father had commemorated the occasion by staying drunk the entire week, and Melanie had cried herself to sleep every night. Their part-time housekeeper, Mrs. Murphy, had tried to make things more normal by bringing in a Christmas tree, but no one had felt like decorating it. The tree had gone to the curb the day after Christmas, as bare as it had come in.

If only I could get out of Christmas altogether this year! Melanie thought as Jesse turned the final corner onto the Andrewses' private road. What she wouldn't give to have a car of her own, like Jesse, so

11

she could drive off into the sunset, never to return. Or at least not until after New Year's.

"Here you are—door-to-door taxi service," Jesse teased, pulling into her driveway.

She forced a smile and gestured around the black interior of Jesse's red BMW. "This is a pretty nice taxi."

He puffed up proudly. "Best taxi in town."

Why does he always have to do that? Melanie wondered, annoyed. *Why can't he just say thank you like any remotely humble person?*

Then she realized she'd just answered her own question.

Climbing out of the car, she slammed the door hard, hoping it would be a long, long time before she needed to use this particular taxi service again.

There were days when she could almost like Jesse. But there were weeks on end when he drove her absolutely crazy.

Two

" '*Tis the season to be jolly,*" Jenna sang, rummaging through her desk after school on Friday. "*Fa la la la la, la la la la!*"

She loved Christmas. As far as she was concerned, it could be Christmas all year round. Everyone at school was excited about the upcoming vacation, decorations were going up all over town, and the whole house smelled of the gingerbread cookies her mother was baking. Soon there would be parties, and winter camp, and caroling, and presents . . .

The thought of presents froze her dead in the middle of the project she was making for textiles class, one hand on the glue stick and the other on the scissors. She had to get Peter the perfect gift this year. Something really special. If only she knew what!

Oh, well, there's plenty of time. Maybe Caitlin will have an idea when she gets home, Jenna thought, returning to her textiles project: a concept drawing of a child's bedroom decorated with an abundance of lightweight fabric.

I'm getting to be an expert at decorating bedrooms,

she thought ironically as she worked. She had recently fixed up her own new third-floor room, only to do it all over again a few weeks later when Caitlin, her older sister, had moved back into it with her. Jenna had badly wanted her own place, but she had to admit that rooming with Caitlin was working out great. Not only was Caitlin a neater and far more pleasant roommate than Jenna's younger sister Maggie had been, but now that she was working as a veterinarian's assistant she was hardly ever home. On weekdays she never got in before dinnertime, leaving Jenna all the time she needed to do her homework in peace. And even on the weekends Caitlin was always running off to walk Abby, her new dog, or one of the animals boarding at Dr. Campbell's. If anything, Jenna wished Caitlin were around a little more, because when she was they had a lot of fun together.

In her drawing, Jenna added a small round table next to the bed and glued a carefully shaped snippet of pink gingham beneath it, creating a skirted nightstand. Then, just to make sure her teacher understood her intentions, she drew a lamp on top.

It was such a relief that so many of her teachers had assigned do-ahead projects or papers that semester, instead of final exams. Jenna liked to get good grades, and she always studied hard, but she

14

hated the uncertainty of taking tests. A person never knew what teachers might ask or whether they'd try to get tricky. She'd take projects and term papers she could prepare in advance any day.

"Jenna," Mrs. Conrad called from downstairs. "Do you want to decorate gingerbread men? Or are you too busy with homework?"

Too busy to help out with cookies? Her mother had to be kidding.

"I'm coming!" she shouted, dropping her pencil. There were notebooks, textbooks, pencils, pens, scissors, paper, and fabric scraps spread out all over the desktop, and for a moment she considered cleaning up the mess before she went down. Then she changed her mind. Caitlin wouldn't care, no one would disturb her things, and it would all be right there waiting when she returned.

" *'Tis the season to be jolly,*" she sang again, running lightly down the stairs. She'd have to find something extra nice to give Caitlin this year too.

"I'm open! Over here!" Peter cried, stretching his arms above his head. Jesse's pass was so perfectly thrown it hit his hands, and a minute later he was in the end zone again, another touchdown to his credit.

"Altmann, way to go!" Jesse whooped, running to congratulate him. "I'd never have guessed you could play football!"

Peter didn't bother to ask why. With his skinny frame and low-key demeanor, he was used to having people assume he was bad at sports. No one ever gave him credit for having more important things to do.

"Actually, I'm not too great at football," he said. "But I'll bet I could wipe a tennis court with anybody here."

He didn't usually boast, and the size of the group playing touch football that Saturday made his wager especially bold, but Peter had confidence in his tennis-playing abilities. He and his older brother, David, had played frequently before David had gone off to college, and David had made his college team easily. Considering that he had beaten David at least half the time, Peter was sure he could have made the CCHS team—if he'd been willing to give up Junior Explorers, which he wasn't.

"Tennis, eh?" Jesse cocked a speculative eyebrow, making Peter wonder if he was about to issue a challenge. He hoped so. If Jesse was any good, it would be fun to have a tennis partner again. Peter was already thinking about where they could get a court when Jesse smiled and shook his head.

"Let's just stick to football, okay? We're creaming them." He spun around and ran back toward the center of the field. "Huddle up!" he bellowed, summoning his team for a strategy meeting.

Peter crowded together with the rest of his teammates, their breath steaming in the cold winter air. Between Eight Prime and friends, they had mustered two even teams of ten, although Chris's team had five girls and Jesse's only four. Jesse surveyed his gang now as he barked out his instructions.

"Barry, you kick off," he directed, nodding toward another member of the school football team. "Kick short. Tanya, you and I'll get out in front and try to recover it ourselves." Despite his earlier reluctance to include girls in the game, Jesse had been quick to capitalize on the exceptional speed of Tanya Jeffries, one of Melanie's friends from the cheerleading squad. Tanya and Melanie were dressed like reverse twins: Tanya in a blue shirt over a red one, Melanie in a red shirt over a blue one, and both in jeans and white running shoes. Melanie smirked at Jesse now, as if to say she'd told him so.

Jesse ignored her. "Peter, Nicole, and everyone else, spread out in the backfield. Don't let them through if they catch the kick. Ready? Break!" The "everyone else" Jesse referred to included Courtney Bell, a new friend of Ben's named Mark Foster, and two of Miguel's water polo buddies, Roger and Joe.

Peter trotted to his assigned position, but his mind wasn't on the kickoff and his eyes weren't on the ball. Instead he gazed down the field at

Jenna, wishing he were losing with her on Chris's team instead of winning on Jesse's. Chris and Maura had managed to stay together on one team, as had Leah and Miguel, but Peter and Jenna, and Courtney and her boyfriend, Jeff Nguyen, had been split up in the selection process. Another Wildcat named Gary Baldwin, cheerleader Angela Maldonado, Caitlin Conrad, and Ben completed Chris's team.

Barry kicked the ball and Jesse and Tanya streaked down the field, the rest of the group fanning out across the grass behind them. The kick went slightly wild and a lot farther than it was supposed to, wobbling toward the left back corner. Peter trotted forward a bit, watching as the ball fell straight toward Jenna's waiting arms.

Catch it! he thought, not caring that she wasn't on his team.

She did, and with a pleasantly surprised expression began running up the sideline. Managing to elude Jesse and Tanya, who were too near the center of the field, she ran directly toward Peter. For a moment he considered pretending to slip to let her go by. Their eyes met and held. Her cheeks were pink; her mouth was open and laughing.

He hesitated, then lunged, tagging her down at the last possible second.

"Peter!" she squealed. "You weren't supposed to catch me."

"Sorry," he teased, still feeling the way the soft gray fleece of her sweatshirt had compressed beneath his fingers. "You were too good to let go."

"Peter!" The rest of her face turned as pink as her cheeks as she took in his double meaning.

The teams were lining up for their next play when a shrill voice cut the air. "Jesse! Hey, Jesse!"

Peter turned his head to see one of the Junior Explorers, Jason Fairchild, charging out onto the field. Mrs. Brown, the first-grader's foster mother, waved apologetically from the sideline.

"Time out!" Jesse called, making the sign of a *T* with both hands. He and Peter walked over to Jason while everyone else took the chance to rest and get a drink.

"Jason, what are you doing here, bud?" Jesse asked, bending down to speak to his pint-sized admirer. "Do you know you're in the middle of a game?"

"Yes, he does," Peter said reproachfully. "I told him we were going to be playing this afternoon."

"I wanted to see you play, Jesse," said Jason, ignoring Peter. Reaching up, he grabbed a handful of Jesse's green jersey. "Is this a real Wildcats shirt?"

Jesse smiled. "As real as they get. It's the one I wore this season."

"Wow," Jason breathed. "Can I play with you?"

"You mean *now*?" Jesse laughed and shook his head. "You'd get squashed."

19

"No fair!" Jason whined, clenching his hands into fists. "I wanna play."

"I told you this morning it was only big kids," Peter reminded him. He realized now that he shouldn't have mentioned the game at all, but Jason had asked about Jesse. The boy hadn't said much at the time—he must already have been busy working on his plan to get his foster mom to bring him back to the park.

"I'm a good player!" Jason protested, flexing a scrawny arm to show off his nonexistent muscle.

"You and I will toss the ball around some other time," Jesse promised.

"When? At winter camp?"

"I'm not going to winter camp, bud. That's just for you Junior Explorers."

"Peter's coming."

"Peter's in charge."

"Jenna's coming."

"Look, Jason, I'm not going to stand here arguing with you." Jesse glanced away, toward the restlessly milling group of would-be football players. "There isn't room for me at winter camp. You guys only have two cabins and they're both full."

"You can have my bed and I'll sleep on the floor."

Jesse shook his head. "Dreamer! You're already sleeping on the floor. Look, Peter, you explain it to him. I have to get everyone back on the field before they cool down and want to quit. See you later, Jason," he added before he struck off across the field.

"You can make room, can't you, Peter?" Jason begged, his light blue eyes wide and pleading. The sprinkling of freckles that usually dominated his nose and cheekbones had faded into a winter paleness so extreme that his skin was nearly as light as his white-blond hair.

Peter shook his head. "I really can't. I know you like Jesse a lot. But Chris and I are going to be there. And Ben. You like Ben, don't you?"

Jason made a face.

"My dad will be there, too, and five of you boys," Peter added. "That's almost too many people already."

"I want Jesse," Jason insisted stubbornly. As if on cue, tears welled up in his eyes and two perfect drops slid off his lashes, making tracks down his cheeks. The sight melted Peter's resolve as nothing else could have. He'd never seen the little bruiser cry before, although Jason's troublemaking ways had caused plenty of tears on the part of others.

"Aw, Jason. Don't cry," he begged, crouching down to hug him. "I didn't know it meant so much to you."

Jason only cried harder. Peter looked helplessly toward Mrs. Brown, who was already on her way over.

"Jason, darling, what's the matter?" she asked, laying a hand on his back.

"Don't call me darling!" Jason snarled, twisting

21

away from her touch while still clinging to Peter. "I'm a boy!"

"Of course you are, dear. I—"

"I'm not a deer!" Jason shouted through his sobs.

Mrs. Brown looked taken aback, but not completely surprised. "I'm so sorry," she apologized to Peter. "If I'd had any idea he was going to behave this way, I never would have brought him."

Peter comforted the crying boy as well as he could. "I guess he's pretty disappointed that Jesse won't be coming to winter camp."

As if to reinforce that conclusion, Jason let out another howl.

Mrs. Brown sighed. "When the social worker placed Jason with me, he was supposed to get a Big Brother. But there are too many kids on the list, and too few men who volunteer their time. I thought Junior Explorers would help, and it has. But one morning a week just isn't enough. Jason needs a father. If only . . ." Her voice quavered and she let the sentence drop. Peter knew she was a widow, and he could guess what she'd meant to say.

Jason's sobs finally settled into hiccups, and Peter turned him over to Mrs. Brown. She nodded good-bye and led Jason off the field by one unresisting hand, his head hanging in defeat. Peter watched him go with a lump in his throat.

So what if we're wedged in cheek to elbow? he reproached himself. *It's only for three nights—we can find a spot on the floor somewhere. Besides, we'll be outside for hours every day.*

Quickly, before he could talk himself out of it, Peter ran over to Jesse.

"You ready?" Jesse greeted him. "Okay, everyone—"

"No, wait. Jesse, why don't you come to winter camp with us? It would mean a lot to Jason."

Jesse looked skeptical. "You said there wasn't room."

"I know. And I won't lie—it's going to be tight. It's just that I've never seen Jason cry about anything before, and I hate to—"

"Jason was *crying?*"

"Didn't you see?" Peter asked incredulously. "He was bawling his eyes out."

"Just because I wasn't coming to camp?"

"That, and . . . well, I think it's a lot of things," Peter hedged, reluctant to say too much about Jason's situation.

"Where is he now?"

"His mom took him home. Look, Jesse, do you want to come? I wish you would."

Jesse thought it over, his conflicting impulses clear on his face. After a moment, he shook his head. "You don't need me there. I feel bad that

23

Jason was crying, but he *is* just a kid. Two minutes into his first snowman he'll forget all about me."

"I'm not so sure."

Jesse made an impatient gesture. "He will. He probably already has."

Peter wanted to argue, but Jesse was yelling for the huddle. "Come on, you guys, let's go!"

Biting back his protests, Peter joined the circle with the others. *Maybe it's for the best*, he thought as Jesse barked out his instructions. *Jesse doesn't want to go, and we really are short on space. Maybe Jesse's right and Jason will forget all about him.*

Somehow he doubted it, though.

"Nicole!" her mother's voice called from somewhere far away. Then again, more insistently: "Nicole, wake up!"

"Huh? what?" Nicole said, struggling upward through layers of sleep. "I'm awake."

Her mother peered down at her, her bright blue eyes sharp with annoyance. "Now you are. You slept right through Pastor Ramsey's sermon."

Nicole stiffened and looked quickly around the church. Sure enough, the pastor had left the pulpit. Not only that, but people were beginning to file out. The service was over.

Nicole turned to her father, seated on her other side. "I only closed my eyes a minute," she protested. "I'm pretty sure I heard the whole thing—or all but the very end."

"Oh, really?" said her mother, leaning back into the bench as if she had all the time in the world. "Then give us a little summary. I'm sure this will be fascinating."

"Fine. Well, he, uh, started off reading something from the Bible. Then he, um . . . talked about it."

Her mother's frosted pink lips formed a hard little line. "*What* did he read from the Bible?"

Nicole strained to remember. She had definitely been awake then. In her mind, she could picture Pastor Ramsey hunched over the lectern, his head bobbing slightly as he droned on and on. She closed her eyes, trying to focus the image. She'd heard the passage—she knew she had. If only someone would give her a hint . . .

She took a stab. "The New Testament."

"That's not funny, Nicole," her father said in an unusually severe tone.

"I'm not trying to be funny, Dad. I just—I don't know why I can't remember, okay? But I absolutely heard that part. As far as the sermon goes, well . . . maybe I was asleep a little longer than I realized. It's just that I'm so exhausted from school. You know we have finals next week, and all the teachers are working us double-time to make up for the vacation."

The church had all but emptied. Nicole turned back to her mother. "Shouldn't we be picking up Heather? Sunday school must be over."

Mrs. Brewster ignored the question. "I don't think it's school that's wearing you out. You've just been too busy lately. We allowed you all those evenings and weekends with Eight Prime because it was such a worthy cause, but now that you kids have the bus, I think you ought to slow down. And there's certainly no reason to be out with Courtney on school nights, the way you were last week."

"We were Christmas shopping, Mom! That's a *very* good reason."

"Not when you're falling asleep in church, it isn't. I guess we're going to have to establish some earlier hours for you, so that you can get some more sleep."

Nicole's eyes widened. "Are you talking about a *bedtime?*"

"It wouldn't kill you."

"Not much! And besides, it's not my fault! If Pastor Ramsey wasn't so boring, I wouldn't have fallen asleep. If you want to know the truth, I don't hear three-quarters of what he says even when I'm awake. And I try to pay attention. I really do. If the church honestly expects us to listen to the sermons, they ought to hire someone who isn't so ancient."

26

Her mom and dad were staring in disbelief, but Nicole tossed her head defiantly. There was no one left in church to overhear her remarks, and her parents had practically forced her into making them. She rose to her feet abruptly.

"So, are we picking up Heather or what?"

Three

"Jenna, this is excellent! Very well thought out," Ms. Harris said when Jenna turned in her final textiles project on Monday.

Jenna beamed at her teacher's praise. She had already liked the decor she'd designed, but knowing she was going to get a good grade made her like it even more. She watched proudly as the teacher checked the quality of her sewing on the skirted nightstand cover she'd made as part of the assignment. Each student had had to sew one thing from his or her drawing to better illustrate the concept and to show the ability to execute it. Jenna had picked the pink gingham nightstand cover because her sister Sarah had liked it a lot, and she planned to give it to her as a Christmas gift.

Christmas! Jenna grinned as she walked back to her seat at one of the long work tables in the home ec room. There were less than two weeks to go before the holiday, and only one week of school. Not only that, but in this class at least, she could coast from now until Friday. She picked up a scrap of red felt and began cutting it into pieces.

"What are you making?" Pam Edwards asked from the seat beside Jenna's.

"I have no idea," Jenna replied happily. "Some sort of Christmas decoration, I guess."

"I can't believe you turned in your project so early. Did Harris like it?"

Jenna nodded. "It's smooth sailing from here on out. All I have to do now is look busy and stay out of trouble."

Pam laughed. "Think you can handle it?"

"I'll do my best."

Everyone settled down to their projects for the day, and somebody switched on the radio. But instead of the usual playlist, a Christmas carol filled the room. Smiles broke out all over, and everyone began bustling around with new energy, seeing the vacation light at the end of the tunnel. Jenna got up to find some green felt and the fabric glue.

I wonder if I could sew Peter a present this year? she thought, still elated by the success of her final project. There wasn't much time. She had to come up with presents for her parents and the rest of her sisters, too, and with winter camp starting almost as soon as school let out, she was already going to be rushing like crazy. Yet she liked the idea of giving Peter something she'd made herself.

Maybe I could sew him a shirt. A flannel shirt. Plaid

flannels were a CCHS staple for cold weather, but they were also worn year-round as lightweight jackets. The more Jenna thought about it, the more she liked the idea.

Cutting out a wreath-shaped piece of green felt, she began gluing circular bits of red fabric to it. *But do I sew well enough to make a button-down?* she worried. She'd never attempted anything quite that ambitious before.

A moment later, she shook off her doubts. Hadn't her final textiles project just been a total success? And sewing that table skirt had been a piece of cake—she'd hardly had to rip out any seams at all.

I'm ready, she decided with a smile. *I'll buy the fabric after school.*

On the first day of Hanukkah, Leah's parents always came home from work early, but she was still surprised to see them both already in the living room when she arrived from school.

"Am I late?" she cried, checking her watch in dismay. She'd stayed after classes to study with Miguel, but she'd expected to be home before her parents.

"Not at all," said her father. "We were just relaxing a little."

They sat on the sofa, drinking tea from glass mugs. On the table in front of her father rested the

Hanukkah menorah and a box of spiral-twisted candles in different colors. The freshly polished menorah gleamed, and Leah smiled at the sight. The winter days were short—soon it would be dark enough to light the first candle.

She poured herself a cup of tea and sat down with her parents.

"Your grandfather called," Mr. Rosenthal said.

"Already?"

Her father's father lived in another state, so they rarely saw him, but they always called him on holidays. The calls were part of their family tradition. And even though Leah's father no longer attended synagogue, he believed in tradition. Tradition showed respect, he'd say, for the people who'd gone before. "And," he'd always add, "Mother would roll over in her grave if we didn't show proper respect."

"I think your grandfather's a little busy tonight," Mrs. Rosenthal told Leah with a wry smile. "But he said he'd try to call again later."

"Busy with what?"

Her mother's smile grew broader. Leah's father rolled his eyes.

"Apparently he's been invited for latkes and sour cream by a widow who lives in his building. He may not get back to his apartment for a while."

"Grandpa has a date?" Leah exclaimed, astonished.

"He sends his love," her father said. "And a check. It's on the way."

Leah smiled. "Grandpa has a date. Wow. I can't *wait* to talk to him now!"

Her father shook his head. "I don't know how big a deal it is—it's only for latkes. And you know your grandfather. He never met a latke he didn't like."

"Neither did I," said Leah, feeling her stomach rumble. "When are we having ours?"

"As soon as we light the menorah," her mother replied.

Mr. Rosenthal glanced at the front window. "It's dark enough now. Are you ready, Leah?"

"Sure." Leah chose a blue candle to place in the farthest right position on the nine-branch menorah, signifying the first night of the eight-day holiday. For the shammes, the center candle that would be used to light the others, she selected white.

Mr. Rosenthal carried the menorah to the window and put it on the sill as his wife and daughter looked on. Then he struck a match and touched the flame to the shammes.

"Go ahead, Leah," he said.

Leah recited the first traditional blessing: "Blessed are you, Lord our God, King of the Universe, who has sanctified us with his commandments and commanded us to kindle the Hanukkah lights."

Her father removed the shammes and brought the burning wick to the candle on the end, lighting it as well. As he did, Leah recited the second blessing, which spoke of a long-ago war and an outnumbered band of Jews, the Maccabees, who triumphed over a cruel oppressor.

"Blessed are you, Lord our God, King of the Universe, who performed miracles for our ancestors in those days, at this season."

Her father carefully replaced the shammes. The third blessing followed, the one said on only the first night.

"Blessed are you, Lord our God, for keeping us alive so we may celebrate this festive day."

The three of them stood silent a moment longer, watching the candles burn. On each day of Hanukkah another candle would be added, until on the last day nine flames—eight plus the shammes—filled the window with light.

"Let's eat," Mr. Rosenthal said, snapping them out of their trance. "How about those latkes, Arlene? Did you remember to buy the applesauce?"

"Of course," Leah's mother replied, put out. "I hope I know what I'm doing after twenty years of marriage."

Mrs. Rosenthal had learned to make the fried potato pancakes from her mother-in-law before the older woman died, when Leah was only a toddler. Since then she'd been carrying on faithfully with the latkes, practicing and perfecting them until Mr.

Rosenthal declared that in another twenty years they'd be almost as good as his mother's.

"You know, Grandma would have made that applesauce from scratch," Leah teased her mother. "She would have picked the apples, too, and probably planted the tree."

"Your grandmother would have grown the sugar cane," Mrs. Rosenthal replied tartly.

"And the sour cream," Leah continued. "How would Grandma do that? Milk a cow?"

Her mother finally cracked a smile. "Oh, please, Leah. You don't just *milk* a cow. First you have to deliver a breech-born calf single-handed, preferably in a storm in the middle of the night, and raise the poor scrawny thing into the most prizewinning cow in the state. *Then* you can milk it and make sour cream."

Leah giggled. "My mistake." She glanced at her father, who was grinning too.

"Sure. Make fun of my poor mother." He tried to look serious enough to assume an air of injury.

"Oh, no, dear," his wife protested, her good humor fully restored. "We were making fun of you."

Mr. Rosenthal followed her into the kitchen. "Well . . . that's all right then."

Leah smiled as they walked off, then turned her attention back to the Hanukkah lights.

Ever since she was little, she had looked forward

to lighting the menorah. As a child, she had simply found the candles pretty, the potato pancakes delicious, and the gifts her family exchanged after dinner a perfect ending to the evening. Gifts weren't a major part of Hanukkah, and the Rosenthals' gifts weren't extravagant—a sweater, some books, a college bond—but they were always from the heart.

As Leah had grown older, though, the flames of the candles had begun to be much more to her than just pretty lights. The ceremony was a way to connect with her Jewish heritage and a chance to reflect on her religious beliefs—Jewish, Christian, or otherwise.

This year, however, as Leah gazed at the candles and tried to sort out what she believed about God, her thoughts returned again and again to the idea that as soon as the menorah went back on the shelf, her mother would break out the Christmas decor. The thought made her vaguely uneasy. In the past, Leah had always been able to separate her father's Jewish traditions neatly from her mother's Christian ones. It had been easy when she'd thought of them only as traditions, actions apart from beliefs. But this year the boundaries were blurring, and she wasn't sure why.

Maybe because I've been so wrapped up with Miguel, she thought, *and how emotional he is about faith.* Leah was used to musing about God with her intellect, but she'd seen Miguel search with his heart.

Or maybe I'm just getting older. Going through the holiday motions might be okay for a child, but Leah wasn't that young anymore, and she was too smart not to see her own inconsistencies. She had always assumed that one day, after studying them all, she'd pick her own religion. Now that seemed so simplistic—as though God could be fit into one set of rules, if she could only figure out whose. And wouldn't she lose something of herself no matter how she chose?

Leah stared at the Hanukkah lights and imagined a huge Victorian Christmas tree covered with glowing candles. In her mind, the two images superimposed and blurred together. Hanukkah and Christmas had nothing to do with each other, but in a sense they were both about light.

Are Christianity and Judaism really so very far apart? she wondered. *Isn't God God?*

"This is hopeless." Melanie sighed, tossing her mother's Bible aside on the bed. Between the tiny type, the whisper-thin paper, and the horribly old-fashioned English, she'd never encountered a tougher book in her life. And then there were all those numbers everywhere, cluttering up the pages until a person could barely see. . . .

Melanie slouched down until her head sank into the pillows. *I should have listened to Peter,* she thought. He'd warned her that the King James Version wasn't the easiest reading. He had even offered to lend her a special study Bible in a modern translation. But Melanie had stubbornly insisted on reading the very copy that had belonged to her mother—and on starting with page one.

And what for, anyway? She didn't remember anymore.

When she'd found the Bible in a bottom drawer of her mother's art studio, hidden like some sort of clue, she'd just felt sure it was important. She'd known her father probably wasn't even aware that the book existed, let alone that it was in the house, and the feeling that had come over her when she'd first opened the leather cover had been eerie, as if her mother were suddenly very near. In some way Melanie must have believed that if she only read the exact same words and turned the exact same pages, she could connect with her mother again.

The whole idea was stupid. She saw that now.

For one thing, she didn't know if her mother had ever even read the Bible. The book could easily have been sitting untouched in a drawer since her mom had peeled off the gift wrap at age fifteen. For another, even if Mrs. Andrews had read it, she obviously hadn't believed what it said. At least not by the time Melanie was born.

Had she ever? Melanie wished that she had asked her, that the two of them had at least talked about religion. *Really* talked about it, not just joked. The only serious things Melanie could remember her mother saying were all along the lines of "Oh, I don't believe that," or, "If God existed, I'm sure he wouldn't run things like this." She couldn't remember ever asking her mom *why* she didn't believe the things she didn't—or, for that matter, why other people did. She'd just taken her mother's pronouncements at face value. Melanie had been such a little kid then, with no idea she was about to lose the chance to ask forever.

Forever. The word could still twist her heart halfway out of her chest. She couldn't believe she'd never see her mom again. Her mind knew her mother was dead, but her heart . . . her heart just refused to accept it. How could it, when all around her everything else seemed the same? Same house, same town . . . She'd never even seen her mother's grave.

She hadn't *wanted* to see it. After the car accident, everything had happened so fast. Her mom's parents, her sister, and a few other relatives had come to the hospital but had arrived too late to say good-bye. There had been only an hour or so after the paramedics had rushed Mrs. Andrews to the hospital—an hour so painful that Melanie refused to remember it.

Then, suddenly, it had been over, and everyone had been whispering about "arrangements" and "the body." Melanie had caught only snatches of the conversation through her brokenhearted sobs, sobs that had risen to drown out the sound of such callousness. Her father had been as quiet as she'd been loud, paralyzed by his grief. Eventually the relatives had grown impatient. First had come the requests, then the demands, that Mr. Andrews inform them of the arrangements. In the end, he had given them back their daughter, to do with as they liked.

Melanie's mother had been buried in southern Iowa, where the rest of her family lived, but Melanie and her father hadn't attended the funeral. Mr. Andrews thought funerals were an appalling custom—painful to the living and of no use to the dead. His refusal to attend, and to bring Melanie, had deepened an already existing rift in the family, and Melanie hadn't seen any of those relatives since. She didn't really miss them—even before her mom had died she'd barely known them—but more and more she regretted not going to the funeral.

Not that she'd had any choice in the matter. Still, the thought of seeing that big, gaping hole in the ground, her mother being lowered into it, the soil thudding down on the coffin . . . Even now her eyes squeezed shut against the pain of the imagined scene.

But maybe if she had seen it, some mental door would have closed for her that was still standing halfway open. Maybe if she'd run her hands over the headstone and squeezed the earth of the grave between her fingers, it would have made things more real somehow. And then, maybe now, when she closed her eyes and wondered where her mother was, she'd know.

Rolling onto her side, Melanie pushed herself up off the pale pink bedspread and wandered across the room to her enormous walk-in closet. One of the white louvered doors was ajar. She pulled it open and drifted inside. Somewhere she had a card . . . somewhere . . .

Taking a shoe box down off the top shelf, she opened the lid and sifted through its contents, barely remembering the item she was looking for. Her fingers paged slowly through the old cards and papers. Nothing. Putting that box aside, she took down another, her fingers moving more quickly as her search became more urgent. At the bottom of the second box she found it—a plain white card printed with small black script. A funeral announcement. Her mother's funeral announcement.

Her mother's only sister, Aunt Gwen, had sent it to her. At the time, Melanie had found the act unspeakably cruel. Every black-on-white word had wounded, and she hadn't seen any reason to send an announcement to people who had already said they wouldn't come. She'd wanted to rip the card to pieces, but instead she'd thrown it into a box at the back of her closet and never looked at it again.

Until now. Now she studied the card in her hands as if seeing it for the first time. It didn't say much. On the front were the words *In Memoriam*, and inside a few simple lines gave a time and date for the burial service. There was no clue to explain why finding it now had suddenly seemed so important. Slowly she flipped the card over. On the back, a simple line drawing gave directions to the cemetery.

And beneath that was an address. . . .

Four

"I should have gotten up five minutes earlier and made my lunch today," Peter grumbled, eyeing the untouched cafeteria tray in front of him with distaste.

Jenna smiled sympathetically, but Ben leaned across the table to point at a gelatinous lump near the top of the tray. "What are you talking about? Look, they made red-and-green Jell-O!"

Peter's lip curled slightly. "Are you sure that isn't the meat loaf?"

Ben's friend Mark laughed. "No, the meat loaf is *gray* and green. Red and green would be their spaghetti."

"Ugh. Thanks for the clarification." Peter stabbed the dense gray slab of meat with his fork.

"You want half?" Jenna offered, holding out a perfect triangle of her thick homemade sandwich.

Salami, cheese, and lettuce peeked invitingly from between two oversized slices of bread, and Peter felt his stomach rumble. "Thanks, but you go ahead," he said, not wanting Jenna to end up hungry. Instead he took a determined bite of meat loaf.

Jenna shrugged and put the sandwich down. "I can't believe it's almost vacation," she said, glancing around the noisy cafeteria. At every table, people seemed to be discussing the same thing. "Ben, did you tell Mark about our winter camp?"

"Every detail," Mark answered quickly, with a slight roll of his eyes. "Please, don't get him started again."

"I didn't tell you *that* much," Ben protested. "I don't even *know* that much. By the way, Jenna, do you think I should bring an extra sleeping bag? And what about long underwear? How many pairs are you bringing?"

"Don't you think that's a little personal?"

Ben blushed. "I didn't mean . . . oh, wow . . . I only . . ."

Peter smiled and tuned Ben out, his thoughts turning instead to a carefully folded paper bag in the zippered front pocket of his backpack. He'd gone Christmas shopping the day before, and although he hadn't had a lot to spend, he'd found something perfect for Jenna: a small silver pin in the shape of a dove. He was so sure she was going to love it, he could barely wait to give it to her. His hand wandered behind him now, toward the pack on the floor beneath his bench.

43

No. You have to wait, he told himself firmly, forcing his hand back to his lap. *You don't want to give it to her in front of Ben and Mark. Besides, if you did, what would you give her on Christmas?*

Immediately he thought of all the other things he'd seen at the mall and known she'd like. He'd love to give her the dove pin now and something else later, but he had gifts to buy for his parents and David, his older brother, and he only had so much money. Reluctantly he picked up his fork and started eating again.

Someday, he thought dreamily, with a sideways glance at Jenna. *Someday I'll give you everything.*

"I can't believe we're wasting an entire afternoon in the library," Courtney Bell moaned, pushing her red hair off her face with both hands.

"Personally, I'm surprised you could find the place," Nicole said. "Did somebody give you directions?"

"Oh, sure." Courtney's voice was sarcastic but unruffled. "You're the *queen* of the library, Nicole. I'll bet half these seats are permanently molded to the shape of your butt."

Nicole couldn't think of a comeback. "We're not getting anything done," she pointed out instead.

"I don't know why we're bothering anyway. Finals are so absurd. You do time in some class every day for a whole semester, then they expect you to get totally worked up about one stupid test at the end. It makes no sense."

"It makes more sense than failing." But Nicole didn't pick up her book either. Courtney hadn't even mentioned the cruelest part—that the tests fell right before Christmas, when all anyone could think about was vacation.

"So what should we do on Saturday?" Nicole asked, leaning back in her seat. "I'm sleeping in till noon, but do you want to go to the mall after that?"

"I'm going out with Jeff Saturday night."

"So what? You're going to be getting ready all day?"

Courtney refused to rise to the bait. "I suppose I could squeeze you in for an hour."

"Give me a break, Court."

"Let's go to the mall on Sunday," Courtney said. "And Monday we'll do something too. I'm pretty sure there's a party Tuesday night."

"Tuesday? Why Tuesday?"

"Why not Tuesday? It's vacation all week."

Nicole shrugged, but the idea of a holiday party was exciting. She'd wear her earrings that looked like miniature Christmas lights, and probably her cropped red sweater with—

"I want to see that new movie, too," Courtney said. "*Deadly Contact.*"

"Ooh! No, the Ethan Ryan one. We *have* to see

that, Court—probably twice. And what about *As I Lay Dreaming*? That looks really good too."

Courtney smiled. "With two whole weeks off, there's no reason we can't see *everything* twice. Now that the God Squad finally got its stupid bus, you can go out every night."

Nicole's answering smile was a little weak, but she wasn't about to tell Courtney her parents' differing viewpoint on that subject. Courtney had been mad enough when she'd found out Eight Prime wasn't breaking up. Nicole didn't even want to imagine what she'd say about a vacation curfew. She could only hope her parents weren't uncool enough to actually go through with that.

"You know what we ought to do?" Courtney asked. "We ought to set up another double date."

"Not a chance," Nicole said immediately. "No way."

"Aw, come on," Courtney wheedled. "You aren't still holding Guy Vaughn against me."

"Until I die." Courtney's last idea for a double date, a blind fix-up between Nicole and a friend of Jeff's, had been a total disaster. Not only was Guy the most completely boring person Nicole had ever met, later he'd had the nerve to say she wasn't someone he'd want to date again.

Like he'd have gotten the chance! Nicole thought, fuming anew at the insult.

"I told you he was a loser," Courtney reminded her. "This time I promise to find someone good."

"Thanks, but I'll pick my own dates from now on. That way I can make sure they're human."

"Oh, come on. Guy was a drag, but he wasn't bad-looking. You're just bent out of shape because he dumped you before you got the chance to dump him."

The truth hurt, but Nicole wasn't going to admit it. "Look, Court, just stay out of my love life, all right?"

Courtney's green eyes glittered with barely suppressed laughter. "What love life?"

"If I'm going to that stupid U.S. Girls thing," Leah told her parents over dinner Tuesday night, "I have to fill out the forms. They have to be postmarked by Thursday."

"Do you mean the California finals?" Mrs. Rosenthal looked perplexed. "I thought you'd decided to do that a long time ago."

"I guess."

Her father laughed. "Don't overwhelm us with enthusiasm, Leah."

Leah put down her fork and looked past her parents to the menorah in the window. There were two candles on the right side now. "It's just that I never wanted to do any of it. I mean, being a glorified clothes hanger isn't exactly one of my dreams."

"No, but attending a good college is," said her

mother. "You know, Leah, with them choosing only five girls out of fifty, no one can say the odds are in your favor. But if they look at academic achievement at all, then your odds get a lot better. In any event, I don't see how you can walk away from this contest now. It's too good an opportunity to throw away, even if you don't like everything about it."

Leah knew her mother was right. She picked up her fork again and took a bit of couscous. In her depressed state it tasted like sand.

"Besides," Mr. Rosenthal added, "a free trip to California in winter can't be all bad."

"About that," Leah said, swallowing her gritty mouthful, "I have to tell them who I'm bringing as my three guests. You two, obviously, but that leaves one spot."

"You should bring a friend," her mother said. "How about one of the girls in Eight Prime?"

Leah shook her head. "That's not going to work. I've already thought about it, and there's no way I can ask one without asking the other two. It would be too uncomfortable."

Mr. Rosenthal nodded. "I see your point. Could you pass the bread?"

Leah handed him the basket, knowing it would be useless to tell him the person she really wanted to take was Miguel.

"I've been thinking of asking Daryl." Daryl Holiday had been her best friend until she'd moved to Chicago. "It would be great to see her again."

"How would she get to St. Louis?" Mrs. Rosenthal asked.

"That's kind of the tricky part," Leah admitted. The contest rules specified that each contestant could bring three guests, but the entire party of four had to fly together out of the same airport. Since the Rosenthals would be leaving from St. Louis, Daryl would have to meet them there. "She'd probably fly from Chicago to St. Louis and hook up with us at the airport somehow."

"I don't know," Mr. Rosenthal said. "That's going to be an expensive lot of fooling around for only a three-day trip, and I doubt Daryl's folks will go for it. Besides, you're going to be pretty busy anyway, aren't you? It's not like you'll get to spend a ton of time together. It would be better to pick someone from school who can ride to the airport with us."

"Yeah." The problem was there was no one else she wanted to ask. "Maybe Grandma would want to come."

"On a plane? To California? Without Grandpa?" Leah's mother laughed. "It's a nice thought, honey, but there's no point even asking."

"Then let's just the three of us go. There's no rule that says we *have* to be four."

"Well, that might be easier," Mrs. Rosenthal said slowly. "If you're sure it's what you want . . ."

"It is," Leah said, suddenly positive.

Why would she want a friend to witness the most embarrassing moment of her life?

" 'For shirt B,' " Jenna read, " 'use pieces one, two, three, four, five, six, seven, and eight.' " She looked up from the pattern instructions to the mess of tissue paper strewn about the folding sewing table in front of her. "Hmm . . . that would appear to be all of them."

Turning back to the instructions in her hand, she tried to figure out how to arrange the pattern pieces on the fabric. "Oh, wait. Some of these pieces have to be cut out of fabric *and* interfacing."

Jenna had never used interfacing before, and for a moment she was tempted to skip that step. Since she was making the shirt for Peter, though, she wanted to do things right.

"How hard can it be?" she muttered, moving the tissue paper pieces onto her bed to make room for the clean-smelling flannel she had purchased and preshrunk the evening before. She'd found the perfect shirt pattern and the perfect plaid for Peter, in shades of light blue and tan. The colors would go great with his blue eyes and blond hair, and Jenna imagined him looking very woodsy and outdoorsmanlike in her creation.

"Let's see," she said, thinking aloud. "The material is forty-five inches wide . . . if I fold it like this . . ."

She wrestled the fabric into position on the table, doing her best to line up the edges. Then, following the diagram in the instructions, she pinned down the pattern piece for the back of the shirt. She had the front piece half pinned down too before she realized she had a problem.

"Oh, great." She groaned. "Now the plaid isn't going to match at the side seams." She'd have to move the front piece, but to where?

And then another problem occurred to her. *The pockets.*

The front of the shirt had two patch pockets. She'd have to cut them out so they lined up exactly with the plaid on the front pieces or they'd look terrible. *Maybe I should leave them off. . . . No. Guys always use their pockets.*

She paused uncertainly, a pin in her hand and several more between her lips. Sewing this shirt was turning out to be a lot more complicated than she'd expected. It was bad enough that she had cuffs and a collar and buttonholes to deal with—she'd known about all that—but she hadn't counted on interfacing, and working with plaid was starting to look like an adventure in itself.

Jenna grimaced, then shrugged off her doubts. *I'll just have to cut out the pieces one at a time,* she thought. *That way I can put them next to each other as*

I go along, to make sure they line up right. Her strategy was a bit of a gamble. In textiles class they'd learned to always pin down all the pieces before cutting anything out to make sure there was room.

"Well, this isn't textiles class. Besides, I bought a little extra, just to be safe."

She reached for the scissors and nervously prepared to make the first cut. "Here goes nothing."

Five

The moment Melanie got home from school that Wednesday, she knew she was in for a terrible evening. The first thing that caught her eye was the Christmas tree in the living room.

Dropping her backpack, she dragged her feet across the marble and the white carpeting to the tree. "I begged Mrs. Murphy not to do this again."

The housekeeper obviously hadn't been listening, because now Melanie stood before a perfect noble fir, running her fingertips over its pliant green needles. The tree was smaller than the one they'd had the previous year, but more beautifully symmetrical.

What a total waste, she thought. Now she and her father would both have to pretend they didn't see it until the twenty-sixth, when he would drag it outside still bare, the way he'd done the year before.

Melanie brought her fingertips to her nose, closing her eyes as the scent of fresh pine exploded in her nostrils. The smell brought back so many memories. . . .

Opening her eyes abruptly, she stepped away

from the tree. *I wonder which room Dad's drinking in.* Because he was definitely drinking. She'd known that the moment she'd walked in the door and seen Mrs. Murphy's handiwork.

She found him in the den, sprawled on the sofa with a beer can in one hand and the remote in the other. A black-and-white Western filled the television screen, but Mr. Andrews's eyes were focused above the set, somewhere off in space. "Did you have a good day?" he asked, not glancing in her direction.

"Better than you," she said bitterly.

He looked at her then and punched the TV volume down a few notches. "What's that supposed to mean?"

"I think you know."

"I'd rather hear you say it."

"I'm tired of . . . of *this*," she said, gesturing impatiently around the room. "There has to be more to life."

He put down the remote, but not the beer. "If there is I haven't found it."

The words were like a slap in the face. How could he say that to her?

"Maybe you haven't looked," she shot back. "Did you ever think about that?"

Before he could answer, she spun on her heel and stalked off down the hall. Running up the marble stairs to her room, she threw herself down on her bed. It had been over two years since her mother's death, but not only wasn't her father getting over it, anyone could see he had just given up.

Not that she'd done much better. Melanie rolled over and pulled a pillow on top of her head. She'd managed not to give in to drinking. Other than that, her life was as empty as his.

And I can't say I've really looked either, she thought, flinching at the admission. It had been all she could do just to survive the last two years. Searching for any type of meaning beyond that had seemed like a luxury.

She thought suddenly of Peter, so different from her—so secure, so full of direction. Whether he was right or wrong in his faith, she was sure he'd never felt so hollow.

Does everyone who doesn't believe in God feel as empty as I do? she wondered. *No. They couldn't.* She remembered feeling fine before her mother had died. She'd been content with the world then. She hadn't questioned anything, hadn't felt anything lacking. She'd believed in her mother, in the safety of her family. She'd believed in life, in love, in herself. . . .

That's the problem, she realized. *It's not that I don't believe in God. It's that I don't believe in anything anymore.*

Nicole sank luxuriously into the mountain of pillows she'd piled at the head of her bed and flipped a page of *Modern Girl* magazine. She was supposed to be studying for her last three finals, and all around her a litter of textbooks, handouts, and handwritten notes attested to that fact. She'd actually even worked for an hour or so. But in the end, thoughts of the impending vacation had so overwhelmed and distracted her that she'd decided to take a study break with her latest magazine.

HOLIDAY PIZZAZZ! read the headline of a major article. EVERY LAST DETAIL FOR AN UNFORGETTABLE FIRST IMPRESSION. Nicole's thin lips pursed with interest as she prepared to read the text opposite a full-page picture of a beautiful girl with a drop-dead-gorgeous guy. They were both dressed to perfection, kissing beneath the mistletoe in a room with a roaring fire.

Nicole couldn't resist imagining what it would be like to be wearing that black velvet gown. The fire would be warm on her bare shoulders, but not as warm as the arms wrapped around her. For a moment she pretended they were Jesse's, ignoring the fact that she'd supposedly given up on him. Then, with a sigh, she shook off the fantasy and tried to imagine something more plausible. What she needed was someone as cute as Jesse, someone as cool, but someone who actually liked her. Someone who appreciated her and wanted to be more than just friends. Someone—

"Hey, Nicole!" Heather cried, bursting into her

bedroom. The door flew open wildly, smacking the wall hard. "Wait till you hear what—"

"Get *out* of here, Heather!" Nicole screamed, outraged. She leapt off the bed and tried to push her thirteen-year-old sister out of the room.

"Don't you want to hear—"

"Don't you want to knock?"

"Man! Get worked up, why don't you?" With a quick shuffle-step left, then right, Heather dodged Nicole's outstretched arms and flopped belly down on her bed. Books and notes went everywhere, but Heather seemed not to notice as she immediately zeroed in on the magazine Nicole had hastily shoved beneath a pillow.

"Studying hard?" she asked, lifting *Modern Girl* out by two fingers.

Nicole glared at her with her hands on her hips, her pulse still pounding from her sister's rude entrance. "If you don't put that down, I swear I'm going to—"

"All right, all right. Get a grip." Heather tossed the magazine aside. "Guess what? Greg is teaching vacation Bible school!" Greg was the Sunday-school teacher Heather had been obsessing over for months. "I'm so excited!"

"You would be," said Nicole, gathering her schoolwork into piles.

"I can't wait. It's six days long, and kids are coming from churches all over town. And here's the best part: It's called Teen Extreme, and it's for teenagers *only*. Isn't that cool?"

At sixteen, Nicole was far beyond being excited by such trivia. "Yippee. Be still, my heart."

Heather's gray eyes narrowed. "I'm going to tell Greg you said that," she threatened.

"Be my guest. What do I care?"

"Well . . . it could be pretty embarrassing for you, sitting in his class every day after he knows what you said."

Nicole carried a stack of papers to her desk. "Ha! That'll be the day. Like I'd waste my vacation at Bible school! You go right ahead and bore yourself to tears. I'm going to sleep in, and go to the mall, and see movies with Courtney, and stay . . ."

She trailed off uneasily as she caught sight of her sister again. Heather was sitting cross-legged on the bed, a huge smirk on her face.

"What?" Nicole asked suspiciously.

Heather only shrugged mysteriously. "Talk to Mom lately?"

"About what?"

Her sister didn't answer, but her lips pressed more tightly together, as if she were fighting back a laugh.

"About what?" Nicole heard the growing desperation in her voice. The way the little creep was acting, she had to know something. But what?

What in the world could Heather find so hysterically funny? Nicole couldn't imagine.

Then she looked into her sister's smug, openly mocking eyes . . . and suddenly knew the answer.

"Oh, no!" she gasped.

"Oh, yes!" Heather cried, abandoning all attempts to rein in her laughter. She crossed her arms over her ribs and rolled around on the bed, cackling as if she'd never heard a better joke.

There was only one thing her sister could mean.

"*Mom!*" Nicole screamed, horrified.

"I wish you didn't have to go in so early," Miguel said, pulling his car over to the curb in front of Leah's condominium. "We didn't even cover those last three chapters."

"Is that why you want me around?" Leah teased. "To quiz you on your biology?"

Miguel smiled mischievously. "Among other things."

She hated the thought of going inside and spending the rest of the evening without him, but she knew she had to. There was no escape.

"Well, hold that thought until Friday night," she said reluctantly. "In the meantime . . ." She leaned across the emergency brake and kissed his tan cheek. The barest hint of stubble tickled her lips before he turned his head, meeting her mouth to mouth. Her heart beat faster and her skin tingled everywhere it touched his. At last she pulled away.

"Friday," she repeated breathlessly. "Or maybe tomorrow, if you ask real nice."

She got out of the car quickly, before he could change her mind, and hurried into the lobby of her building. In the elevator, she checked her watch—7:30.

"Great," she muttered. Her parents were working late that night, so she and Miguel had studied at his house, then gone to Burger City. The annoying part was that her mom wouldn't have minded if she'd stayed out a couple more hours. But she couldn't— she had to do that stupid thing for U.S. Girls.

Heading straight to her room, she flipped on her computer, glared at the screen a moment, and then attacked the keys.

" 'What Being a U.S. Girl Means to Me,' " she read aloud, centering her newly typed title at the top of the screen. "Not much."

She felt like typing that, too, but somehow restrained herself. She couldn't believe she was wasting her time with such a stupid essay when she could be studying for her biology exam with Miguel— or, better yet, studying Miguel. But if she was going to be in the modeling contest finals, her application had to be postmarked no later than Thursday, and she'd put it off until Wednesday night.

Mainly because I couldn't bring myself to write this garbage, she thought disgustedly. She didn't mind having to write an essay—on the contrary, she *liked* writing essays—but of all the stupid topics . . .

"I should have gotten some tips from Nicole." Nicole was certain to know exactly what type of mush the judges were looking for.

For the hundredth time, Leah thought what a shame it was that Nicole hadn't won instead of her. On the other hand, Nicole's main interest had been the chance to model—and all the glory and fame she seemed to think would go with the job. She'd been far more enthusiastic about the free facials the winner would get than about any college scholarship. Fifteen thousand dollars a year in tuition money would be wasted on Nicole unless there was some sort of radical shift in her priorities.

I'll bet she could have written a killer essay, though—all about how pleased and honored she is to represent such a cool store and such a great product.

Leah frowned. Heck, she could write that essay too. The difference was Nicole would have meant it.

"I won't do it."

Scholarship or no, she had to draw the line somewhere. How could she ever respect herself again if she stooped to their level? Sighing, she stared at the title on the screen in front of her.

And then she had an idea.

"Oh, wow," she said with a chuckle. "Why didn't I think of this before?"

Her course was obvious. She would not write a gushy tribute to the thrills of modeling blue jeans. What she'd write instead was an essay on American patriotism.

"Now there's a subject I can get into," she said, hands hovering over the keys. All she needed was a hook, a truly great opening line.

"Got it!" she exclaimed happily, and her fingers began to fly.

Six

Melanie's pencil moved quickly as she finished the next-to-the-last essay question on Mrs. Gregor's third-period U.S. history final. *A normal teacher would have been content with a term paper*, she thought, *but not Mrs. Gregor.* The crusty old history teacher had assigned her papers early, to leave time for a final too.

To her credit, however, the test had been pretty fair. Anyone who had read the chapters and paid the slightest attention in class should have been able to handle it. As Melanie read the final question she was already feeling the dual relief of being nearly finished and knowing she'd done well.

What is the Second Amendment to the Constitution, Melanie read, *and what current debate revolves around it?*

She smiled. The Second Amendment was Gregor's pet subject and therefore impossible not to know by heart. Melanie pounced on the last blank space on her exam, sinking the period at the end of her final sentence with a flourish.

Done! Even better, she knew she'd aced it. Leaning back in her chair, Melanie savored the accomplishment. Gregor's had been her last final. From here on out, she'd simply be filling up chairs until vacation started.

"If you are done with your exam, kindly bring it to the front of the room," Mrs. Gregor said in the bellowing whisper she saved for exam days. Melanie and just about everyone else got up to carry their test papers forward. "The rest of you have five minutes."

Melanie glanced at the clock as she slipped back into her seat, surprised to see that the teacher was calling in the papers before the end of the period. On the other hand, nearly everyone was already done, and there was no point in dragging out the inevitable for a few people who obviously hadn't studied.

One of the slackers was Lou Anne Simmons. Melanie watched sympathetically from across the aisle as her fellow cheerleader frantically scribbled a very long answer across the back of one of her test pages—a sure sign she didn't know the answer and was trying to bogus her way into partial credit. Another teacher might have fallen for it, but not Mrs. Gregor.

"Okay, time's up!" Mrs. Gregor called.

Lou Anne simply wrote faster, until a significant look from Mrs. Gregor let her know she'd better quit fooling around. She slid sideways out of her seat and shuffled up to the teacher's desk, still writing.

"How do you think you did?" she asked Melanie worriedly when she sat back down. The entire class was talking now, free for the rest of the period.

"All right, I guess," Melanie replied cautiously, not wanting to make Lou Anne feel worse.

"I did okay on everything except that stupid procedure for proposing and ratifying an amendment." Lou Anne shook her head impatiently. "Who cares anyway? It's not like we're ever going to *do* it."

Melanie laughed. "No. Probably not." Although it should have been obvious the question would be on the test. "What do you think we'll do in cheerleading practice today?" she asked to change the subject. "I wonder if Sandra will want us to practice our basketball cheers, or if we're just going to fool around."

Lou Anne shrugged. "Fool around, I hope. I don't even know why we have to practice today, what with vacation coming up. It's a total waste of time."

Melanie considered defending their cheerleading coach's decision, then decided to let it go. She knew Lou Anne was only parroting something Vanessa must have said—behind Sandra's back, of course. That was strictly Vanessa's style.

"Has Vanessa said anything to you about me?" Melanie asked Lou Anne point-blank. Since Jesse had dumped Vanessa, Melanie could only wonder what lies the vindictive senior was spreading about her. She certainly wasn't saying anything to her face—she wasn't speaking to her at all.

"Um . . . well . . . like what?" Lou Anne asked, squirming uncomfortably in her chair.

Melanie watched her a minute, then shrugged. "You know what? Forget it. I don't want to know."

She should have known better than to ask Lou Anne an honest question. The way Lou Anne constantly brown-nosed Vanessa, her loyalties should have been obvious. Melanie faced the front of the room again. Lou Anne and Vanessa could have each other; Melanie didn't need them. Tanya and Angela were on her side, and Sue Tilford and Cindy White stayed mostly neutral. Tiffany Barrett was a world-class pain in the butt, but then she always had been. At least Tiffany spread the grief around.

"Melanie!" Lou Anne whispered, trying to get her attention again. "Vanessa will calm down. She's just a little upset right now."

And what's her excuse for the rest of the time? Melanie felt like asking. Instead she flashed Lou Anne a brief, fake smile and did her best to forget the whole thing. Lou Anne would be all right—if she ever found a spine.

Only a minute remained before the bell. Melanie let her eyes wander over the walls of the room, where Mrs. Gregor had taped, pasted, and tacked a unique assortment of holiday decorations. Santas and elves rubbed elbows with menorahs and dreidels. Christmas trees and stockings alternated with pointy New Year's hats and HAPPY KWANZAA! signs. And like a running theme throughout were angels— angels of every size, color, and description. Mrs. Gregor collected them.

"I don't want you to think I'm being partial with my angels," she'd explained the day she'd hung them up. "Because not only are angels important in Judaism, Christianity, *and* Islam, even nonbelievers like them. Besides," she'd added with a rare smile, "they're pretty."

Well, some are, Melanie reflected as she waited for the bell to ring. Coming from all different cultures and periods of history, some verged on the bizarre, and a few were even scary. Melanie's eyes skipped from one to another with increasing restlessness.

Her mother had liked angels too. She'd never thought much about it before, but it seemed an odd preference now. *Maybe she just thought they were pretty, like Mrs. Gregor said. Maybe they were as big a fairy tale to her as Santa Claus and his flying reindeer.* Maybe she hadn't even known that angels were important in three religions.

Or maybe she had.

Melanie sighed. She wished she knew.

* * *

"Well . . . the thing is, the plaid on these fronts doesn't match," Caitlin said slowly, examining the unfinished shirt Jenna had thrust into her hands. Caitlin had just come home from work and was still wearing a smock printed with cartoon cats and dogs, but Jenna hadn't been able to wait even a second for her sister to change clothes.

"I know!" she said impatiently. "That's what I want you to help me with."

Caitlin looked dubious. "Help you how? I can't change the fabric."

"Just tell me what I ought to do! I mean, there has to be a way to fix it, right?"

Caitlin handed the flannel back to Jenna. "Plaids are tough. If you don't cut them out right, you're kind of stuck."

"Are you saying I need to start over?"

Caitlin made an apologetic face. "Do you have more fabric?" she asked timidly.

Jenna sat down hard on her bed. She had been so careful to line up the plaid at the side seams. It had never occurred to her to worry about the two edges of the front, where the shirt buttoned. Now the plaid did a stutter-step across the closing, repeating where it should have continued.

Caitlin slipped out of her smock, revealing a pink thermal undershirt underneath. "It's not as bad as all that," she said. "You don't have to redo

68

the whole shirt—just replace one side of the front. Do you have enough fabric for that?"

"Maybe." Jenna was miserable at the thought of so much extra work, but at least she'd figured it out before she'd put on the collar and sleeves. "I guess."

Caitlin walked over and examined the shirt more carefully. "I don't think it will be that much trouble," she said, reading Jenna's mind. "Bring out your extra fabric, and we'll see if we can find enough for a new front that lines up."

Between them they laid out Jenna's biggest scrap, Jenna thanking her stars she'd had the foresight to buy extra cloth. Caitlin went to work with the pattern piece, and gradually Jenna relaxed. Her sister seemed so sure of what she was doing that it was impossible not to trust her.

So what if I'm taking a little step backward? she thought. *It's only Thursday night. I have plenty of time.*

"How are things going at work?" she asked while Caitlin pinned. "Anything new?"

"Actually, yes. Today a lady with a greyhound asked Dr. Campbell if we could walk it for her during the winter. She has arthritis and the cold makes it worse, but if the dog doesn't get out to run, he chews up everything in sight. Or so she says. Personally, I can't imagine such a bad dog."

She took a moment to smile at Abby, who had

obediently curled up in her lilac-colored dog bed the moment they'd entered the room.

"Who's going to walk it?" asked Jenna. "You?"

"Yes. But not for Dr. Campbell. He said he's busy enough without going into the dog-walking business, but that if I want to I can arrange something with her on my own—like a side job. He said I could put up a notice on the board in the waiting room, too, and probably get a few more dogs from elderly clients."

"Caitlin, that's great! Think of the extra money you'll make!"

Caitlin shook her head. "It won't be all that much. Besides, it's not about the money. I'm just so glad to finally be working."

"Even so, it won't be bad having some extra cash with Christmas on the way. I still don't even know what I'm going to buy everyone, do you?"

"Well, yes," Caitlin admitted. "Except for Mary Beth. She ought to be the easiest, but for some reason this year she's the hardest."

Jenna didn't want to hurt Caitlin's feelings, so she didn't point out that it was hard to think of a present for someone you never saw. "Mom said Mary Beth won't be home until the twenty-third this year," she said instead. "I guess she's skiing with college friends."

Caitlin nodded. "That's only for a few days,

though, and then she's going to spend the whole rest of the vacation with us. I can't wait to see her."

Jenna's lips compressed. *I hope you see her more than you did over Thanksgiving,* she thought. When their older sister had come home in November, she'd been more interested in running around looking up old friends than in spending time with Caitlin. They'd done a couple of things together, but Mary Beth hadn't seemed to realize how much Caitlin had been looking forward to her visit. She'd spent as much time with Maggie as with the sister who had once been her favorite.

"Peter's brother is coming home late too, on Christmas Eve," Jenna said abruptly. "I can barely remember the last time I saw David."

"Fourth of July. He was here for the parade."

"That's right. Boy, you have a good memory."

"Not that good," Caitlin mumbled, turning red. "Here, uh, I'll just check this plaid one more time, then I think we can cut this piece out."

"See you next year!"

The farewell rang out above the other noises in the crowded main hall and was taken up all over. "Next year! See you next year!" ecstatic students shouted as locker doors slammed everywhere.

Peter stood patiently to one side while Jenna rooted around in her own gift-wrap-covered locker, gathering up her things. "I can't believe it's really here," he said to the back of her head. "Vacation at last!"

Jenna turned around eagerly, a smile on her face and small tissue-wrapped gifts in each hand. "I know. Isn't it great?" She put the packages into the unzipped backpack at her feet and continued with her locker. Out came a jar of fancy bath crystals, a tin of peanut brittle, a funny little Santa made of red foil-wrapped candies glued together with some cotton . . .

"What have you got in there?" Peter asked. "Where did that stuff come from?"

"Friends," she answered vaguely. "You know." She stopped packing suddenly, as if struck by some horrible thought. "I mean, you got stuff too. Right?" she asked anxiously.

Peter smiled. "How much of that stuff came from guys?" he countered, gesturing toward her full backpack.

"Well, uh . . . none."

"Exactly. And except for you, all my friends are guys."

Her smile gradually reappeared. Turning back around, she took a small red-and-green bag from her locker and held it out to him, grinning. "Speaking of which, here you go, friend."

"What's this? We're doing our presents now?" Far from being cheered by the prospect of a gift, Peter's heart sank as he took the bag. Not only had he removed Jenna's pin from his backpack the day before, he'd been looking forward to giving it to her somewhere a little more romantic than the holiday-trash-strewn main hall.

"That's not your Christmas present, silly," Jenna said with a laugh. "It's only some gingerbread men I made you."

"Gingerbread men?" Peter eyed the sack with new appreciation. "And if you're giving them to me now, then it must be okay to—"

"Go ahead. They won't be much good if you wait until Christmas."

Peter extracted a thick, delicious-looking gingerbread boy with raisins for buttons and shorts made of icing. He hesitated a moment, then bit off a red-booted foot. "Ooh. Good," he said, taking another bite. "*Really* good."

He held out the bag to Jenna as she closed her locker door. "Do you want one?"

She pulled a face and put a hand over her stomach. "Don't even ask me how many of those I've had in the last two days. Not to mention that all we did in any of my classes today was fool around and eat junk food."

"Yeah. My teachers were in a good mood too." The hallway was nearly empty, abandoned as quickly as it had filled. "Ready to go?"

Jenna nodded and hoisted her loaded pack onto

one shoulder. "It seems weird in here now, doesn't it?" she said as the two of them walked toward the main exit. "I mean, I've been in the hall when it was empty before, but it never felt quite so . . . deserted."

"It's the vacation. It feels even stranger on the last day in June."

Jenna shivered a little, shaking off the strangeness. Then Peter pushed the exit door open and both of them shivered for real. The temperature had dropped into the twenties, and the first snow flurries of the season skittered fitfully across the prematurely darkened sky.

"Brrr!" Jenna said, huddling into her coat. "*Now* it feels like Christmas."

The cold bit at Peter's nose, and he buried his hands in his pockets as they headed toward the student parking lot. Jenna's cookie bag bounced along at his side, suspended from his wrist by twin string handles.

"This is more like it!" he said happily. "I was starting to think we wouldn't have snow for winter camp, and that would have been terrible."

"Terrible," Jenna repeated with a wry smile. "It would have been a crying shame to stay warm and dry all that time."

Peter knew Jenna wasn't crazy about cold weather, but he also knew she was kidding. The whole idea of winter camp was to let the kids play in the snow.

"So you'll drink some extra hot chocolate," he teased. "I know how much you'll hate that."

He could think of a better way of keeping Jenna warm, but he was too embarrassed to ask if he could put his arm around her. Even though they were supposedly a couple now, Jenna still acted as if they were only friends when it came to anything physical. They held hands occasionally, and they'd hugged a couple of times, but she always seemed so tentative, so uncomfortable. They'd never even repeated that first brief kiss he'd surprised her with at the park.

Peter sighed and shoved his hands deeper into his pockets as they neared the parking lot. It wasn't as if he wanted anything really intimate. He knew she believed in waiting for marriage, and he believed in that too.

It would just be nice to kiss her once in a while, he thought, sneaking a look at her profile. Jenna's round cheeks were pink from the frosty air, and her long hair blew around her like a soft brown cloud. *Better yet, it would be nice if she'd kiss me!*

He let them into his car, started the engine, and turned on the heater full blast. The windblown snow that had fallen hadn't been enough to accumulate on the windshield, and the few flakes that had stuck gradually disappeared under the assault from the defroster. As Peter watched them melt, his mind returned to the Junior Explorers.

"I wish we had three cabins instead of two," he blurted out. "Then we could have invited all of Eight Prime to come with us."

Jenna looked puzzled. "I didn't get the impression that anyone other than Ben really wanted to come."

Peter put the Toyota in gear and began driving through the icy parking lot. Jenna was right—they hadn't exactly clamored to be included. And if he was honest, Peter had to admit there was really only one other member of Eight Prime he particularly wanted to be there: Jesse.

The truth was that he was worried about Jason. The boy had always been a handful, but lately he was downright hard to control. In addition, something about his pranks and fooling around was changing. Whereas in the past he'd gotten into trouble mostly to create a little excitement, lately he was getting time-outs for reasons ranging from pulling Cheryl's hair to starting a fistfight with Danny.

"I wish Jesse were coming," Peter muttered. Having Jason's idol around might have helped to calm him down.

Jenna touched his arm. "Don't worry about Jason. He'll be fine."

Peter took his eyes off the road to stare at her. "What? Do you have ESP now?"

She laughed. "It wasn't that much of a stretch. I know you're worried about him, and why else would you want Jesse there? It's not like he's your best friend."

"I like Jesse."

"Maybe. But *I'm* your best friend. And don't you ever forget it." Her smile was wide and flirty as she gave him a mischievous wink.

Not likely, Peter thought, his heart beating faster. He was sure he'd never forget even a single thing about Jenna for as long as he lived.

Seven

"Have fun!" Mrs. Brewster cried through her cracked-open car window. Waving, she drove off down the street.

"Yeah. Sure," Nicole said bitterly. She could have said more—a lot more—but she didn't trust that stringy-haired little traitor Heather not to repeat every word the moment they got home.

Whenever that might be. It wasn't bad enough they had to attend some heinous Bible class at the crack of dawn. Mrs. Brewster hadn't even let Nicole drive them there. Carless, they were doomed to wait for Mommy to come pick them up, just like the rest of the babies who couldn't find more productive ways to spend their vacations.

If this is supposed to make me like church better, it's having the wrong effect, Nicole thought rebelliously, following Heather up a walkway to a door with a bright green TEEN EXTREME poster on it. The class was at a conference center downtown so that kids from all over could attend without giving preference to any specific church. But instead of being excited by the prospect of meeting new people, Nicole found fault with that too. *They probably needed to invite the whole stupid state just to fill the stupid room*, she thought sullenly.

Heather opened the door and a blast of warm air hit them in the face. In spite of her irritation at being there, Nicole found herself hurrying inside just to escape the cold. The snow flurries of the day before had blown themselves out overnight, but there was no sun shining that Saturday morning, and the sky overhead was as flat and gray as the deck of a battleship.

Inside, Heather shrugged off her parka eagerly and grabbed a hanger from the jam-packed coat-rack to the right of the door. "Come on," she said. "Take off your coat and let's sit down."

Nicole simply glared.

"Fine. Be that way," said Heather, hanging up her coat. "See ya." She walked over to the nearest row of tables and chairs, where she was greeted by delighted squeals from a few of her Sunday-school friends.

Nicole reluctantly let her coat slide down her shoulders as she watched Heather's tight little group. *Those kids can't all be thirteen. Some of them look like they've still got training wheels on their bikes.* Nicole was almost certainly the oldest person in the room. And as if that weren't bad enough, the group was seventy percent female.

Not that I'd ever glance twice at some pimply little junior-high-school boy. She dropped her coat on the floor at the end of the rack, hoping it would get trampled to the point where her mother had to buy her a new one. Small payback for six wasted days of vacation, but she'd take what she could get.

Then, still barely able to believe she was there, Nicole shuffled toward a vacant chair at the end of the very last row. Everyone else in the room was milling around, laughing and visiting, but Nicole didn't plan to socialize. Besides, she wanted to get a seat in the back while the getting was good. She slipped into the chair she had chosen, declining to meet the eyes of the people talking around her, and passed the time by surreptitiously taking in her surroundings.

The meeting room Greg had chosen was large and windowless. The carpet was tan, the walls and acoustic ceiling tiles white. For furniture, there were five rows of folding tables, with ten folding chairs in each row. A plain brown lectern and dry-erase whiteboard stood at the front of the room; the coatrack and door were in back. Aside from the poster on the door, there was no clue anywhere that this was a Bible class. They could have been there for a lecture on napkin folding or nuclear science, or anything in between.

On top of everything else, Nicole found herself resenting the unrelieved plainness of the room. *I don't know why we couldn't do this at our church*, she thought. At least there the rooms were comfortable. And so what if the class was open to kids from all different denominations? Weren't buildings neutral?

The door behind her flew open suddenly, making everyone turn around. Greg Lewis bounded into the room and ran up to the front. "Hi, everybody!" he shouted, like the host of some cheesy talk show. "It's great to see you all here!"

Nicole sank a little lower in her seat, but not before she checked to see if Heather was swooning. She was. *Like I had to look*.

"Hi, Greg!" a number of students, including Heather, answered. Nicole was embarrassed for them.

Greg trotted over to the podium, looking like Mr. Clean-Cut in his corduroys and blazer, a collared shirt under his sweater. "Wow, it's great to be here. Are we ever going to have fun!"

Nicole's head went down another inch. *Six whole days to think of a way to get even with Mom . . .*

"Hey, but these rows aren't very friendly! What do you say we move all these tables into a big U shape, so everyone can see everybody else?"

"No!" Nicole blurted before she could stop herself, but her voice was drowned out by a chorus of agreement from the others.

The next thing she knew, a couple of delinquents were dragging her table off as if she weren't

81

even sitting behind it. It wasn't until people started pulling over chairs to sit down in the new configuration, though, that Nicole realized she had a dilemma. There was no way she wanted to sit on one of the arms of that U—it would put her too close to the front. But if she sat on the bottom part of the letter, farthest away from Greg, she'd be right in his line of sight. *It probably doesn't matter either way. Sooner or later, he's bound to ask me something.*

Still, why tempt fate? Standing up and grabbing her chair, Nicole hurried to push it in at the beginning of the curve, the least conspicuous place. She had no sooner taken her seat, however, than Greg abandoned the podium, carrying a swivel chair for himself into the middle of the open area surrounded by the tables.

"I want to be sure I can see everyone," he explained cheerfully as he sat down. "Okay! Let's get started! We've got so many great things planned that I'm just going to dive right in."

People actually leaned forward in their chairs, eager to hear what he'd say.

What a geekfest, thought Nicole. *If Courtney saw me now, I'd die.*

She'd never thought Greg was goofy before. In fact, she'd never have admitted it to Heather, but up until then she'd always thought he was kind of cute. That morning, though, everything he did annoyed her. The way he dressed, the way he smiled, and especially the brisk way he rubbed his hands together as he began describing the Teen Extreme program nearly drove her to distraction.

"Over the next few days, you're going to get to know the Bible better than you ever have," he said. "*Really* know it. Not just what it says, but how it relates to your life, and what scripture means in terms of the decisions you make every day. Along the way, we're going to get to know each other a lot better, too, and probably even learn a few things about ourselves."

Greg did a slow turn in his chair to look at the fifty-odd people around him. "We call this week Teen Extreme because we're going to have some extreme fun. But before we get started, I'd like everyone to put on a name tag."

Nicole wasn't the only one who groaned.

"Just for a day or two," Greg said quickly. "Until I learn who everyone is." He stood up and began passing out the self-adhesive tags. "Could someone maybe help me by doing these from the other end?"

Heather nearly gave herself a hernia straining forward over her table, her arm stretched out in front of her as far as it would go.

"Great. Thanks, Heather," he said, tossing her a stack.

"I have a teen assistant," he informed them conversationally as he continued along the tables, "but unfortunately he got delayed this morning picking up some art supplies. He ought to be here soon, though."

Like we care, Nicole thought, sinking even lower in her seat. Then Greg put a name tag in front of her and she slipped down another notch.

"I think you'll all really like him," Greg said. "He's participated in the program for the last three years, and this year he's going to help lead some of the discussions and focus groups."

Four vacations in a row doing this? Nicole nearly gagged. *Who is this person? Is he completely without a life or what?*

As if on cue, the door burst open again, admitting a tall boy with reddish brown hair and arms full of construction paper and glue sticks. Nicole took one look and wanted to slide out of her seat right down to the floor.

Greg's teen assistant was Guy Vaughn.

"So. Christmas," Tanya said as she and Melanie walked through the entrance of the crowded, gaudily decorated shopping mall on Saturday. "I could take a pass on the entire thing this year."

A relieved smile broke out on Melanie's face. Someone else had dared to say it! She wouldn't have to pretend around Tanya.

Tanya shook her head. "I shouldn't complain," she went on. "I know other kids have it worse. But this year, with the divorce and everything . . ."

"Complain away," Melanie urged, glad to have finally found an ally. "I hate Christmas too."

The two girls wove through the holiday shoppers on their way to the big department store at the end of the mall.

"I don't really *hate* it," Tanya said. "I mean, I didn't used to. But this is the first one since my folks split up, and you can't believe what a war it's turning into. My dad wants us to spend Christmas day at his new place, and my mom wants us with her. They can't work it out, so now they're trying to make me choose." She gave an involuntary little shudder. "I'm not going to choose. No way."

"At least they both want you."

Her comment drew Tanya up short beside a towering cone of red poinsettias—someone's idea of an alternative Christmas tree. "Oh, Melanie. I'm sorry. What an idiot I am to be complaining about my parents when mine are both—"

"No. That's okay," Melanie said quickly, not wanting to hear the end of that sentence. "It's just . . . well, all the holidays are hard. Come on, let's keep walking while there's still a square inch of space to do it in."

She headed toward the end of the mall and Tanya followed silently.

Now she feels sorry for me, Melanie thought. She hated being pitied. Sometimes the only thing that made life bearable was knowing that everyone around her thought she had it whipped. She got by by pretending to be the girl people already thought she was.

"So how are Bryan and Bayley?" she asked brightly, relying on her old faking skills. "I'll bet they're looking forward to seeing Santa Claus."

Tanya laughed, and a little of the tension between them dissolved. "The twins only believe in Santa when they think it'll get them more presents. I have to admit that I'm kind of looking forward to that part, though. They always have so much fun! Last year, they got this walkie-talkie set, and the next thing we all knew . . ."

Melanie smiled and nodded vacantly as Tanya went on with her story. Hearing her friend gush about her younger brothers made Melanie think of Amy, which made her think about Peter and the Junior Explorers, which reminded her of the upcoming winter camp. Suddenly Melanie desperately wished she were going. So what if it was cold and crowded? And never mind the fact that Peter and Jenna's new relationship would be in front of her every minute. At least she'd get to be with Amy and other happy people until Christmas Eve.

". . . and then Bayley ran inside screaming, 'Come quick!' and before we could get to the door, Bryan burst through it looking like the Abominable Snowman. It was hilarious!"

Melanie laughed on cue and Tanya joined in, thinking she'd cheered her friend up.

At the cosmetics counter, Tanya checked out perfumes for her mother. With nothing else to do, Melanie gradually noticed that all the advertising posters featured angels—angels wearing makeup, of course.

Like angels need the help, she thought. Or maybe the customers were supposed to think that wearing makeup would make *them* look like angels. *Sure it will.* Melanie was only fifteen but she was already smarter than that.

There were more angels in the lingerie section. Angels ruled the juniors' section. And by the time she and Tanya left the store, Melanie was seeing angels all over the mall.

What is it with angels this year? she thought irritably. *Are there more of them than usual, or am I just noticing them more for some reason?*

Then an odd chill ran from her neck to her knees, and Melanie knew the answer.

When she'd been in the hospital after her head injury, she'd been half unconscious when she'd thought she'd seen a beautiful blond woman leaning over her bed. The memory had haunted her for days, and although she had managed not to think about it recently, she was sure she'd never forget that sight. Even now the recollection made her skin prickle. Was the figure she'd seen her mother, an angel, or pure hallucination?

Her mother. The familiar pain of missing her stabbed through Melanie's gut again. She wondered if there was snow on her grave yet, way up in Iowa, or if the ground was the same frozen brown as in Clearwater Crossing.

I still love you, Mom, she said silently. *Wherever you are, I hope you know that. And if there was any way I could show you how much . . . well . . .*

I'd do it in a second.

" 'With right sides together, pin sleeve to inside of armhole, taking care to match all symbols.' " Jenna stopped reading the pattern instructions long enough to squint at the drawing supposed to illustrate that step. " 'Stitch, easing sleeve between the notches. Stitch again.' Again? What for?"

The words blurred and swam on the page in front of her as Jenna tried to figure them out. Exhausted, she glanced at the clock: 11:20 P.M.

"How did it get so late?" she groaned. Between church in the morning and shopping for presents in the afternoon, Sunday had just whizzed by. Before she knew it, she was doing the after-dinner dishes. Then she'd had to wrap the gifts she had bought for her family, wash her hair, and pack for winter camp. By the time Jenna's bags were ready and waiting beside the front door, Caitlin was already showering for bed. So Jenna had dragged the sewing machine, its folding table, and all the mess that went with it down to the den so she could work while her family slept. Two complicated cuffs later, she was wishing like anything that she could go to bed too.

If I don't get some sleep, I'm going to be useless at camp tomorrow. She squinted at the instructions again, then rubbed her tired eyes until they watered. *Heck, I'm useless now.*

She considered asking her mother or Caitlin to finish the shirt while she was away at camp. Either of them could probably do a better job than she would anyway. But a moment later she shook her head.

No. The whole point of giving Peter a shirt I made myself is making it myself.

She studied the instructions one last time, then determinedly began pinning a sleeve into an armhole. *Just finish the sleeves*, she ordered herself as she worked. *The sleeves and the buttonholes.*

The rest of the shirt was already essentially complete. The collar was on, the pockets were perfect, and the cuffs she'd just made looked pretty good too. If she had to, once the sleeves and buttonholes were done she could sneak the shirt up to camp to finish at night. Putting on the buttons and making the hem were hand sewing anyway.

Done pinning, Jenna began sewing on the first

sleeve. The hum of the sewing machine sounded like a roar in the otherwise quiet house. Ignoring the noise, she guided the fabric under the needle. She was most of the way around the armhole when the machine slowed down with a groan.

"Come on," she muttered, trying to push the underarm through to be sewn. With all the seams coming together there, that was the thickest part, but even so the shirt seemed to be hanging up on something. The needle went up and down, making stitches, but the fabric didn't move forward. *I'm probably making a big knot*, she worried. Reversing the machine, she tried to back the piece out, but the needle still sewed in place. She was stuck—and all the stitching she'd just put in would be a big loopy snarl of thread underneath that she'd have to rip out before she continued.

Just what I need, she thought, spinning the needle up to the highest position and lifting the presser foot. Impatiently she pulled the shirt toward her, but it didn't budge, hopelessly caught in the mess of bobbin thread underneath. Jenna wiggled it and jiggled it. She tried moving the needle to different positions. But it was no use. She was going to have to cut it loose.

Picking up the shears with her right hand, she used her left hand to pull the trapped fabric up and away from the metal needle plate and began snipping the snarl of thread holding the shirt to the machine. Somehow the combined mess of fabric and thread had become so thick that she could barely lift it far enough to see which part was thread and which was shirt. She cut as carefully as she could, hoping she was only getting thread, but as the seconds dragged into minutes she began to panic and cut faster.

Just get it loose, she told herself. *Get it loose and hurry!* The shears went snip, snip, snip.

Oops.

It was only a seam allowance, she told herself quickly, willing her words to be true. She hurriedly examined the freed shirt, trying to find the bit of fabric she'd just cut through. *It isn't going to show. It isn't going to—*

"Oh, no!" she cried, forgetting that the rest of her family was sleeping. "Oh, I don't believe it!"

She'd cut right through the middle of the back. Somehow the back of the shirt had gotten caught up under the armhole seam and sewn right into her mess. No wonder the fabric had seemed so thick! Jenna blinked hard a few times, as if that might erase the awful sight in front of her. But the damage remained—a hole that could never be patched without showing. She put her fingertip beneath it and saw her flesh peek through the opening. Then her finger went out of focus as her tired eyes filled with tears.

There was no way she could give the shirt to

Peter now. Not only didn't she have a big enough piece of fabric to replace the back, she didn't have the time. Bitterly disappointed, she fingered the hole in the flannel until her tears fell in earnest. The shirt was ruined, the stores were all closed, and in just a few hours she'd be leaving for camp.

Now what was she going to give Peter?

Eight

Nicole wondered what would happen if she just kept walking—past the door labeled TEEN EX-TREME, past the whole cheesy complex the door was part of, and down the road to the pay phone at the convenience store on the corner. If Courtney was awake, maybe she could come pick her up and they could spend the morning at the mall . . . or at Courtney's house . . .

Or driving around in circles. I don't care. Anything would be better than going to this stupid class. Nicole hesitated outside the door, her hand hovering in-decisively over the knob. Her mother had already driven off. *So long as I get back in time, she'll probably never find out. . . .*

"Hurry up, Nicole!" Heather said impatiently behind her. "Why are you just standing there?"

And then Nicole stopped wondering what would happen. She knew. If she kept on walking, Heather would rat her out to their parents the second she got the chance. Nicole yanked the heavy door open and stalked angrily to her chair, sliding her rear along the smooth contoured plastic until her head was as low as possible. She hated Greg's stupid class, she hated her parents for making her go to it, she hated her kiss-butt little sister on general principle, and she hated missing her vacation most of all.

Well, maybe not most of all. She'd forgotten to mention how much she hated Guy.

She glanced at him now, up at the front of the room with Greg, so full of his own importance. *I'd hate him even if he had been interested in me,* she thought, shrugging out of her jacket and tossing her gloves on the floor. *Although maybe not as much.*

No, I would. He's condescending, and boring, and not remotely the kind of guy I'm into.

Still . . . it killed her every time she remembered he'd said she wasn't a serious person. She didn't want him to *like* her—far from it—but the fact that he looked down on her was nothing short of infuriating. At least, she was pretty sure he still looked down on her. They hadn't spoken beyond exchanging short, embarrassed hellos.

For the first time it occurred to her to wonder if Guy was as horrified to see her in his precious program as she'd been to see him. She smiled, kind of hoping he was.

"All right, everyone," Greg called out, clapping his hands to cut through the noise. "We're about ready to get started here, so if you'll all take a seat . . ."

Nearly everyone except Nicole was fooling around: talking, giggling, or acting like the immature little twerps they were. Although, to her surprise, it had turned out that several of the kids were closer to Nicole's age than she'd originally thought.

"Come on, people, let's get started," Guy echoed in a bossy tone.

Gradually the other seats at the tables filled. Heather took her usual spot near the front with a couple of her friends. An extremely thin girl Nicole had envied the first day sat a few seats to their right. There were also some guys, but none worth mentioning, and a lot of faces were hidden to Nicole in her slumped-down position. Directly across from her, though, was the one fellow student Nicole thought she might like to know better—Guy's thirteen-year-old sister, Brenda.

From what she'd seen so far, Brenda was as fiery as Guy was cold, and as cool as he was geeky. Nicole didn't know if she liked her because she reminded her of Courtney, or if because watching her drive Guy crazy was the only fun thing about class.

"I'd like to start out today with a sharing," Greg announced, pulling up his chair.

Nicole had to stifle a groan. A lot of the stuff they did was pretty juvenile—singing, playing games like Bible Trivia, or making construction paper frames to decorate favorite verses—but the activities she liked least were the ones that resulted in having to reveal things about herself: small group discussions and anything involving the word *sharing*.

So far she'd managed to stay silent, or get away with superficial answers like *I love <u>cheese</u>* and *I hate <u>liver</u>*. She'd also learned that neither Greg nor Guy aggressively pursued details that weren't offered freely, so by now she felt pretty safe. Even so, it was awkward when one of them looked at her and she had to pretend not to notice.

She made herself as small as she could and prepared to wait Greg out.

"What I had in mind," Greg began, "is to spend some time this morning talking about the priorities we set and how they ultimately affect us. People have a tendency to get caught up in things that *seem* important but in the end aren't important at all. Things like getting into the most prestigious club, or having the best kind of car, or winning some prize or contest. If we let ourselves, we can put so much energy into those types of pursuits that there's nothing left over for the things that do matter: enjoying our families and friends, helping one anoth—"

"Yeah! Like Nicole!" Heather burst out excitedly, not even waiting for Greg to finish. "You've never seen anyone more completely obsessed with losing weight in your life. Every time I walk into the bathroom, she's either standing on the scale or checking herself in the mirror." Heather's friends giggled.

Nicole sat bolt upright, her heart pounding with outrage and blood rushing into her cheeks. "That's such a lie!" she shot back, not caring that the only lie was her denial. How dare Heather say *anything* about her?

"Oh, please—" Heather began, but Greg broke in before she could make things worse.

"Okay. This is a good subject. Lots of people are concerned about their weight. I'd be surprised if Nicole is the only person here who thinks about that."

"I didn't say she thinks about it, I said she's obsessed," Heather corrected.

Nicole rose a few inches out of her chair before she remembered she couldn't pound Heather in Bible class. She was still trying to figure out some long-distance way to kill her when Brenda Vaughn leapt into the conversation.

"It's hard not to be obsessed when everywhere we look everyone is telling us we have to be thin. You can say what you want about equality, but women are still judged primarily on how they look. Boys don't even care what a girl's like inside, as long as she's pretty enough."

"Oh, baloney," Guy said, temporarily forgetting his neutral role. "Don't blame us for your vanity."

"It's not vanity," the thin girl protested. "It's survival."

"It's stupid," another boy said.

"Oh, so you're saying you *like* fat girls, then?"

"I'm not saying—"

"Well!" Greg broke in hastily. "We seem to have hit a nerve. Instead of arguing, though, let's see if we can put this into a Biblical perspective. Can anyone think of something in scripture that applies to this discussion?"

"That God loves us just as we are," a chubby girl said self-righteously.

"Then he can love us thin just as easily as fat, can't he?" Brenda asked.

Despite her anger at Heather, Nicole's mouth twitched at the corners.

Guy was flipping frantically through his dog-eared Bible, but Nicole didn't wait to hear what he found.

"Everyone obsesses now and then," she said slowly, turning a poisonous gaze on Heather. "It's normal. For example, a girl might get a crush on some completely inappropriate guy. Someone who's *way too old for her*, for instance."

Her words were so loaded with emphasis that everyone in the room had to know she was talking about someone. But only Heather knew who.

"Well, yeah, uh, sure," Heather said, backpedaling frantically. "And besides, I didn't mean you were *obsessed*. I just meant . . . uh . . ." Her eyes begged Nicole to keep silent.

Nicole let her squirm a little longer as she toyed with the idea of revealing her crush on Greg. Then, reluctantly, she decided against it.

For now.

There were three more days of class to endure— and as long as Heather lived in terror of her own secret coming to light, her silence on the topic of Nicole's personal life was virtually assured. If Nicole played her trump card now, though, Heather would have nothing left to fear. She'd be sure to declare open season on every little bad habit Nicole had ever had.

Nicole smiled smugly at her terrified sister, then settled back into her seat.

Maybe on the last day, she thought. *In the last ten minutes of the very last hour . . .*

Heather had better watch out then.

"*Dashing through the snow, in a sky blue Chevy bus, o'er the bumps we go . . .* Oh, I don't know." Jenna giggled as she abandoned her spontaneous singing attempt. "What rhymes with *bus?*"

"*Us*," Amy Robbins said from the seat beside her.

"*Cuss*," said Jason. He was sitting by Peter across the aisle.

"That's not very festive!" Jenna told him, pretending to be shocked. Jason shrugged and turned away.

"Why don't we sing it the regular way?" Chris said from behind the wheel. *"Dashing through the snow . . . ,"* he bellowed, not caring in the least that he was totally off-key.

Soon the entire gang had joined in, and shouted choruses of "Jingle Bells" were bouncing around the bus's metal interior like BBs in a washing machine. Jenna put her hands over her ears, which only spurred the kids to ever-increasing volumes.

Eleven Junior Explorers had ended up coming on the trip. At the last minute, tomboyish Priscilla had been added to Amy, Lisa, Cheryl, Daneesha, and Joy. The boys on board were Jason, Danny, Elton, Leo, and Lars, the last two being brothers who had joined Junior Explorers at the end of the previous summer, too late to go to summer camp. The kids sat spread all over the bus, with Maura, Mr. and Mrs. Altmann, and Ben spaced among them to keep some sort of order.

The impromptu shouting of "Jingle Bells" finally came to an end.

"Almost there!" Chris called back to the kids. His announcement was met with screams of approval that even the adults joined in on.

Jenna smiled as she watched the last few miles of woods pass by. Snow flurries blew against the windshield and dusted the bare trees and pines lining their route through the state park. Then suddenly the bus slowed down.

100

"Here we go!" Chris said, turning down a side road where Jenna saw a small wooden sign that said CABINS over an arrow. The woods, already thick, became even denser as the bus cruised down a long, gradual hill.

"I see them! I see them!" Priscilla cried, leaping out of her seat and running up the aisle toward the front of the bus. The other kids jumped up to follow.

"Everybody, sit down," Peter instructed firmly. But it was a losing battle. He had barely gotten them seated again when the bus rolled off the road and parked in a flat, unpaved area on the side.

"Everybody out for Camp Cucamonga!" Chris called, cranking the handle that opened the bus door. A blast of frigid air rushed in, convincing kids and grown-ups alike to put on their coats, hats, and gloves.

"Camp Cucamonga?" Ben protested, hurrying up to the front, the long tassel on his snowboarding hat trailing out behind him. "I thought this was winter camp!"

Chris turned around, his expression perplexed. "What? No, dude. It's Camp Cowabunga."

"Cowabunga?" Baffled, Ben turned to Jenna for help.

Jason pushed impatiently past Peter, his small figure bulky in a red down jacket, his backpack already on his shoulders. "He's kidding you," he told Ben, his upper lip curled in disdain. "Man, get a grip." A moment later he was leaping out the door, the first one to touch ground.

Ben pulled himself up taller as if to reclaim some lost dignity, then shrugged and ran out the door behind Jason. "First dibs on the good sled!" Jenna heard him shout.

Then Jason's voice, more faintly: "Geez, how old are you, anyway?"

Soon everyone was pouring out of the bus, and the woods echoed with shouts and laughter. Trees stretched in every direction: bushy green pines, and bare oaks and hickories. The only open places were the road itself and the large sloping clearing the bus was parked at the top of. At the other edge of the clearing, a short distance back from the road, Jenna spotted two little brown cabins crouched under the sheltering trees. Some of the kids had already run down the hill to get a better look. The rest gathered impatiently around the back of the bus, where Chris and Peter had opened the rear door and were handing out backpacks, sleeping bags, duffels, and an assortment of boxes, air mattresses, and sporting equipment so extensive it was hard to believe they were only staying four days. Jenna gazed longingly at the cabins, eager to check them out, then wandered toward the back of the bus to help with the unloading. She was only halfway there, however, when she was stopped by a sharp tug on her mittened hand.

"Jenna, I don't feel good," Cheryl whined. "I think I'm going to hurl."

"What?" Jenna cried, alarmed.

Cheryl's head was already bending over. Jumping back just in time, Jenna narrowly avoided having her hiking boots splashed by a steaming, toxic-looking mixture of fruit punch and half-chewed Chee-tos.

"I want to go home!" Cheryl wailed, starting to cry.

"Oh, sweetie." Jenna took the girl's hand again and led her away from the mess. "We just got here. Let's get you some water, and then you can lie down for a minute. Maybe you'll feel better."

"No," Cheryl said stubbornly, shaking her head and crying even harder. "I want to go home now."

Before Jenna could figure out what to do, Mrs. Altmann appeared. "I'll take care of this," she said, putting a hand on Cheryl's shoulder. "Why don't you go help the others?"

"I don't know," Jenna said uncertainly. "She seems pretty sick, Mrs. Altmann."

"You'd be sick too, if you'd eaten all that junk food in the backseat of a bus. She's carsick, that's all. Come on, Cheryl, you can help me set up the kitchen. I bet I have something in my boxes that will make your tummy feel better."

Cheryl looked up with a hopeful expression, her cheeks already returning to their normal color. "Candy?"

"Okay. Now I know you're fine," Jenna said, laughing.

Mrs. Altmann ushered Cheryl off, and Jenna took a moment to kick dirt over the vomit so no one would step in it. The frozen ground was covered with dead leaves, but only the barest hint of snow powdered the open places, accumulating an inch or two deep around tree trunks and bushes.

By the time Jenna had rendered the area safe to walk on, the back of the bus was essentially unloaded. She decided to check the interior instead, to see what had been left behind in the mad rush out the door.

"Jenna! I can't find my mittens!" Elton's plaintive voice greeted her the moment she stepped inside. He was in the back, peering under the seats.

Jenna frowned. Four days without mittens would be impossible with so much outdoor play planned. "Did you bring a second pair?"

"I don't want my other pair. Those were my *lucky* mittens."

Jenna wondered how lucky they could be if they were already lost, but she got down on her hands and knees to help him look.

"I need 'em," Elton whined frantically as they searched. "Those are the best for riding sleds. What'll I do when it starts to snow?"

If *it starts to snow*, Jenna thought. The flurries

that had been blowing through town for the last few days weren't sticking, and they had yet to see anything resembling a true snowstorm. She knew all the kids were excited about the possibility of making snowmen and sledding, and for their sake she hoped it would snow hard. For herself, though, she wouldn't mind an alternate plan of long, rambling walks through the powdered-sugar-dusted woods, followed by hot, hearty meals prepared by Mrs. Altmann. At night there would be cookies and hot chocolate in their sleeping bags, and story after story until everyone fell asleep. And, of course, Peter would be there. . . .

"Oh, wait!" Elton said suddenly. "I think I put 'em in my backpack." He was off before Jenna could reply, thundering down the aisle and out the door.

She picked herself up off the sticky floor and watched through a window as the little boy joined the group down by the cabins. Nearly everyone was there now, milling around out front or carrying things through the wide-open doors. Cheryl was standing on the small front step of the cabin on the right, looking perfectly recovered, while Daneesha tried to drag a duffel bag nearly as large as herself through the door.

As Jenna watched, Peter hurried to help Daneesha with her load. The bag that had been all but impossible for the girl to move went up on his shoulder as if it weighed nothing. Peter had always been strong, but as Jenna watched his back disappear into the cabin she wondered if he wasn't a little broader, his shoulders a little wider, than they'd been the last time she'd noticed. She thought of him as skinny, she realized, but that wasn't quite true anymore.

I hope that shirt's the right size, she thought, before she remembered it didn't matter. She'd wanted to give Peter the best gift ever this year. Instead she'd ended up with nothing.

Just don't get all upset again. She took a couple of deep breaths. Camp lasted only until noon on Christmas Eve, and Jenna had already figured out that she could use those few free hours to buy a new, better present for Peter. The only problem now was figuring out what she could get on such short notice.

She sighed as she rose from the bus seat and headed down the stairs. So far she hadn't been able to think of a thing.

"So what are you doing tomorrow?" Leah asked Miguel over the phone. "Want to get together?"

It was the final night of Hanukkah, and from where she stood at the edge of the kitchen, Leah could see the menorah blazing brightly in the window. Eight candles had been kindled that night, in addition to the shammes. Their combined flames were so pretty that Leah had turned off the other lights in the room.

"Want to go up to the lake?" Miguel suggested.

She laughed. "You're kidding, right? It's snowing outside, in case you haven't noticed."

"Well, we don't have to get out of the car."

"Next idea, please."

"I suppose we could go Christmas shopping, like everyone else in town." He hesitated. "That's okay now, right?"

"This is the last night of Hanukkah, if that's what you mean. It would have been okay before."

Miguel didn't seem to know how to handle the fact that she celebrated both holidays. She had to give him credit for trying, though. Rather than simply ignoring the Jewish holiday, as most of her other friends had done, he'd taken her to lunch at Burger City and given her a card.

"I really wasn't sure . . . ," he'd said as he'd handed her the blue envelope, embarrassment written all over his face. "I mean, if I'm making a fool of myself, I hope you'll tell me. And I didn't know if I should get you a present now, or wait until Christmas, or—"

"Thanks. The card's fine," she'd interrupted. "It's not that big a deal, Miguel. I mean, it is, but it's kind of a family holiday."

He'd seemed relieved.

In a way, Leah was glad Hanukkah was over, so she could go back to being like everyone else.

Except that she wasn't like everyone else. Not everyone else in Clearwater Crossing, at least. And while she wasn't sorry for the difference, she was tired of thinking about it.

"You know what?" she said. "Let's go to the lake after all. I wouldn't mind just getting out of town for a while."

Nine

"Peter, you said we were going to ride the sleds, not drag them around," Jason whined. "The snow's gonna melt."

"Oh, quit complaining." Chris butted in cheerfully. "The sledding limousine isn't running today, so if you want to go, you have to walk."

The other six kids strung out on the path between Chris and Peter giggled, and Jason muttered something Peter was just as glad he didn't catch.

"Walking is good for you," Ben told Jason sagely, earning a dirty look for his trouble.

During the night, a few inches of snow had finally fallen, dressing the woods in white. When the kids had crawled out of their sleeping bags in the morning, they'd been so excited that Peter could barely convince them to put on their clothes and eat breakfast, so eager had they been to throw snowballs at each other and scrape the ground into dirty snowmen.

Jason, in particular, had started in immediately. "I want to sled!" he'd announced, jumping on Peter's back from behind as Peter was rolling up his sleeping bag. "Get up. Let's go."

"I might get up, if you'd get off me."

"You said," Jason had reminded him.

"I said what?"

"That we'd sled if we got some snow. So get up!"

"I didn't say we'd sled in our pajamas. Give me a minute here."

Each of the cabins had two tiny bedrooms, a single bathroom, and a living room with a small adjoining kitchen and dining nook. For the first night in the boys' cabin, Mr. Altmann had taken the bedroom with the double bed, Chris and Ben had taken the twin beds in the other room, and Peter had slept on an air mattress on the living room floor, along with his five junior charges. Shaking Jason off his back, Peter had finished rolling his sleeping bag and pulling on his jeans only moments before a brisk knock had sounded and his mother and Maura had walked in the door.

"Breakfast!" Mrs. Altmann had called cheerfully, a tray of warm cinnamon rolls in her hands. Maura had followed behind with a pitcher of juice and an enormous Thermos of hot chocolate. "Here are your rolls, Peter. Give them cereal, too, if they want it. Everything you need is in your cupboards, and there's plenty of milk in the refrigerator."

She had bustled back out before he could ask her what Jenna was doing. Then, when breakfast was

110

over, the kids had split immediately into a sledding group and a snowman group, and Jenna had opted to stay at the cabins with Maura and the creative types. He'd barely even gotten to say good morning to her before he and his group were trudging toward the sledding hill.

Peter sighed. He hadn't expected romance, but a little contact would have been nice.

"Are we there yet?" Elton asked, startling Peter back to the present. "My legs are tired."

"Almost," Peter reassured him.

"This hill is too far. Why couldn't we just ride the sleds in front of the cabins?" Leo asked for at least the eleventh time. Both Peter and Chris had tired of telling him that the hill there wasn't steep enough, but Ben jumped in again.

"Because we're going to the best sledding hill ever!" he said. "Right, Peter?"

"Right," Peter answered, wishing he were back at the cabins with Jenna. It was a long way to the sledding hill—farther than he'd remembered—and his feet were already freezing. In the half hour they'd been walking, he and Chris dragging the two old-fashioned wooden sleds behind them, the snow had grown wetter and wetter, and Peter's boots were soaked through to his socks.

"Here we are!" Chris cried at last. The trail had broken out of the woods at the top of a ridge. On one side the level land disappeared into more trees, but on the other it fell away in a long, gentle slope that seemed to go on and on.

"Cool!" Priscilla exclaimed, looking eagerly down the hillside. "Can I go first?"

"No, me!" Jason shouted. "It was my idea!"

"There are two sleds—" Ben began, but he was drowned out in the chaos of shouting that followed.

"My turn!"

"No, mine!"

"You always go first!"

"No fair!"

"*I'm* going first," Chris announced. "Then Peter, to make sure the hill is safe." Under cover of the protests that followed, he whispered in Peter's ear. "What do you think? It looks a little iffy to me."

Peter nodded. Patches of brown showed through here and there. Worse, instead of looking new and fluffy white, the snow was the dull gray color of melting ice. "Bare and slushy," he said.

"Do you think we should even try it?"

Peter hesitated, glancing irresolutely over his shoulder at the kids. Jason's wide eyes bored into his.

"We have to," Peter whispered to Chris.

Chris went first on the bigger sled, bumping and jolting on the uneven snow cover. The kids cheered as he took off, but only halfway down the hill the sled ground to a stop, its runners churning up mud. "No good!" Chris called back to Peter, pointing. "Try over that way."

Peter weighed less than Chris, and so did his sled. Moving to the edge of the open area, where the snow looked a little thicker, he launched himself down the slope. For a few seconds it was fun; then hanging on turned into work as the sled began bucking and jerking through both patchy places and wet ones. The sun was shining on the slope, and the farther Peter got from the trees at the top, the slushier the snow became. Two-thirds of the way down, he put his feet to the ground and skidded to a stop, shaking his head. Conditions were not good at all.

By the time he'd dragged the sled back up to the top and rejoined Chris and Ben, all the kids were clamoring for a turn, not in the least discouraged by what they had just witnessed.

"Do you think we should let them try?" Peter asked.

Chris grimaced, then shrugged. "I guess. We're here."

His decision was met with shouts of joy by the Junior Explorers.

"They're a lot lighter than you two," Ben said. "Maybe they'll stay on top of the snow instead of cutting through it."

"They might, if it wasn't melting," said Peter. "If we're going to do this, Chris, we'd better do it fast."

The kids picked numbers between one and twenty

113

to decide the sledding order. Priscilla and Daneesha drew the first turns.

"No fair!" Jason howled. His guess had landed him in fifth position. "You can't let two girls go! It has to be one girl and one boy."

"I'm pretty sure that isn't in my rule book," Chris told him. He flipped through the pages of an imaginary manual hovering in the air in front of him. "Nope. Says in here that I'm *perfectly* fair."

But after Daneesha wiped out in a bare spot and Priscilla went facefirst into the slush, Chris quit joking around. The snow was melting so quickly they could almost see it going. Rivulets of water were tinkling everywhere, and defeated snow slid off the trees with dull thuds. Everything was wet—especially Priscilla and Dani.

"Maybe we ought to call it a day . . . ," Peter began.

Leo and Lars, whose turns were next, didn't like the way the conversation was heading. They took off quickly, before Peter could tell them not to, and both wiped out near the top of the hill, their sleds hung up on obstructions beneath the melting snow.

"That's it," Peter called loudly. "I'm sorry, but that's all for today. Somebody's going to get hurt." Every run of the sleds had left wet, muddy ruts, and a few of the lumpy places were starting to look like rocks.

Priscilla and Daneesha seemed to agree with the decision. Lars and Leo simply wiped their palms down their wet, muddy jackets and began bringing the sleds back up. Even Danny and Elton didn't argue, although they had missed their turns, but Jason positively exploded.

"No way! No fair!" he screamed. "Everyone got to go but me!"

"That's not true," Ben said. "I didn't."

"You shut up!" Jason shrieked. "It's not fair, Peter, and you know it!"

Ben looked stricken. For a moment Peter thought he might even cry.

"Jason, you apologize right now," Peter snapped.

Jason glowered, then dropped his eyes. "Sorry," he muttered sullenly.

"That's better. You can sled first the next time, when some real snow falls," Peter promised. "We'll keep the same order, so you and Danny are first."

"I don't want to go first—I want to go now! What if it doesn't snow again?"

He had a valid point. Peter was tempted to let him wipe out once in the mud, just in case this was the only sledding opportunity. But then he shook his head. He was already having trouble controlling Jason. If he backed down now, things would only get worse.

"We'll just have to hope it does," he replied.

Jason's pale skin was blotchy with rage. "It's all your fault, Peter! You should have gotten up earlier! I hate this stupid winter camp, and I hate you!"

He turned and stormed off down the path toward the cabins before Peter could reply. Gathering his wits, Peter started to go after him, but Chris stopped him with a hand on his shoulder.

"He doesn't mean it," he said. "Just let him walk back on his own. We're right behind him anyway."

"Don't you think I ought to talk to him?"

"Sure. But let him cool off awhile first."

"What do you mean you can't go?" Leah wailed. "I thought it was all settled. I already turned in my stuff!"

Mrs. Rosenthal grimaced from across the dinner table. "I'm so sorry, honey. We had no way of knowing they were going to call a faculty retreat."

"But the contest is over a three-day weekend! They can't expect you to work on a holiday!"

"Technically, you're right," her father said. "*Technically*, attendance is voluntary. But everyone knows they keep track of stuff like this, and it comes back to haunt you later. Besides, I'll be hanged if I'm going to let the department make a bunch of decisions without me."

Leah groaned. "I can't believe this."

Her mother hesitated, then lifted her chin. "I'll

skip it," she said heroically. "Going to this retreat isn't nearly as important to me as the U.S. Girls contest is to you."

"That contest isn't important to me at all! It's just that without you there, it'll be even more horrible."

"Your father can represent both of us, then, and find out what I miss," Mrs. Rosenthal said.

But to her own surprise, Leah heard herself declining her mother's offer. "No. Go to the retreat. You know you want to, and there's no point in all of us suffering."

The hopeful look on her mother's face settled the matter for good.

"The whole thing is chaperoned like crazy," Leah added. "You know I'll be perfectly safe."

Her father nodded. "We trust you anyway."

"Can I be excused?" Leah asked abruptly, pushing back her chair.

"Oh, Leah. You're upset," her mother said.

"No. There's just something I have to do."

"Go ahead," said her father.

Leah walked to her bedroom, her disappointment already lessening. In a way, she was relieved. Part of her had looked forward to having her parents' support, but an even bigger part had realized that having them in the audience, watching her every move, would make her more self-conscious than she already was.

117

It would be better to go by herself, even if it was an atrocious waste of three free tickets to California. In her mind, Leah formulated the letter she was about to write to U.S. Girls, explaining the change of plans.

Hey, wait a minute! she thought suddenly. *That's right! There are three extra tickets now.*

And suddenly she knew what she wanted to do. Running the last few steps to her room, she slid into the chair in front of her computer.

"Dear U.S. Girls," she began, smiling as she typed.

"Sing 'Here Comes Santa Claus,' " Lisa demanded drowsily from her Barbie sleeping bag.

Jenna adjusted the guitar on her knee and looked down at the Junior Explorers. Amy and Daneesha were already asleep, their small heads close together. Joy and Lisa were almost out too, and even stubborn Priscilla looked as though she wouldn't last much longer.

"I think that one's a little too fast," Jenna said with a smile. "How about this one instead?" She strummed the guitar a few times, out of practice but improving fast. *"Silent night, holy night . . ."*

She sang it as well as she could, the way she'd sing it in church on Christmas Eve, and by the time she had finished, every one of the girls was asleep.

Jenna slipped the guitar strap off her shoulder and silently lowered the instrument into its open case.

The stillness in the cabin was absolute, and outside all was quiet too. Maura and Mrs. Altmann were taking their turns sleeping in the bedrooms that night and, judging by the hush, they'd fallen asleep along with the girls. Rising slowly to avoid disturbing the peace, Jenna crossed to the dining nook and took a chair beside the window.

The stars outside were thick and brilliant, and a big moon lit the sky, shining down on the patchy snow. The trees cast shadows so sharp they had substance. Jenna gazed, mesmerized, through the glass, awed by the scene's quiet beauty.

Then an unexpected scuffling behind her made her twist around.

"Amy!" she whispered. The girl had climbed out of her sleeping bag and was standing at the edge of the linoleum in her pink footed pajamas. "What are you doing up?"

Amy frowned. "I can't sleep," she said. "I miss my daddy."

Jenna smiled. "You're just a little homesick, that's all."

Amy shook her head. "No, because I miss Melanie too, and Melanie doesn't live at my house."

"Oh. Well, I know Melanie likes you a lot."

Jenna patted her lap, aware she was a poor substitute. "But since she's not here, do you want to sit with me?"

Amy gazed at her solemnly, then carefully climbed into her lap. "What are you looking at?" she asked, tucking her head full of springy brown curls under Jenna's chin.

"The stars."

Amy nodded knowingly. "Which one is it?"

"Excuse me?"

"The star. The Christmas star."

"I'm not sure I—"

"The star for baby Jesus." Amy wriggled around to meet Jenna's eyes. "Which star is that?"

"Well, uh, I'm not sure."

Jenna had heard various theories about that long-ago star: that it was some kind of stellar explosion that had burned itself out in Biblical times; that it was really several stars that, aligned just right, had appeared much larger and brighter; that the wise men were actually astrologers acting on the relative positions of the regular stars, not following some new one. Jenna wasn't sure it even mattered. The important thing was that somehow the sky had signaled his birth, just as the angels had proclaimed it.

"Maybe now . . . ," Jenna said hesitantly, "maybe now that he's come, they're all Christmas stars."

"We could pick one," Amy suggested. "Let's pick one and pretend."

"All right."

Amy leaned forward until her nose was an inch from the glass and her breath condensed on the pane. "That one," she decided, pointing.

It could have been any of them, it could have been all of them—Jenna couldn't tell by the direction of Amy's small finger. Then suddenly it seemed that one star out that way *was* a little brighter than the others. Maybe it was Amy's star, maybe not. Maybe it was the Christmas star, maybe not.

But it wasn't that hard to imagine it shining out over the Holy Land long ago, inspiring a group of wise men to follow.

Ten

Melanie plopped down cross-legged on the cold carpeting, the unopened box of ornaments in her hands and the bare Christmas tree in front of her. The energy she'd felt a moment before had been completely sapped by the sight of that lonely fir.

"Why did I think I wanted to do this?" she asked, knowing there was no one to hear her. Her father was out in the poolhouse, no doubt drinking his lunch.

" 'Tis the season,' " she muttered cynically. " 'Fa la la la la.' " But she was sure the only reason he'd retreated to the poolhouse in December was to avoid seeing the tree in the living room every time he went to the kitchen for a beer.

And I thought decorating it would make him feel better. She stuck out her bottom lip. Why should she care what would make him feel better? What about what would make *her* feel better?

Not decorating this stupid Christmas tree, that's for sure. Taking it out to the trash, maybe . . .

She flipped the lid off the box she'd brought out

of storage and removed a sheet of bubble wrap. The first layer of hand-blown glass ornaments met her eyes, sparkling as if new. Her mother had loved unique handmade ornaments and had stored them all in special red-and-green compartmentalized boxes. Melanie had grabbed the first dusty box she'd seen. Now she stared at the contents in disbelief.

Angels. A whole, carefully packed layer of them.

She lifted one from its little cell. It dangled lightly in her hand, suspended from a loop of thread as if flying. The figure's porcelain face was ethereally pale, her hair gold, like Melanie's mother's. A long white gown draped down to her bare feet, and delicate, iridescent feathered wings stretched wide over her head. In her hands, she held a paintbrush.

The paintbrush was the final straw. Melanie burst into tears.

Abandoning the box on the carpet, she ran upstairs to her room, barely aware that she still gripped the angel tightly by its thread. When she realized, she threw it away from her, onto the bed. Then, wiping her tears with the palms of both hands, she hurried to her closet and reached under the lingerie in her top drawer.

Pulling out the funeral announcement, she stared down at it through her tears. *I should have gone*, she thought. Maybe her dad was right and her presence at the funeral hadn't mattered to her mother one way or the other. But all of a sudden it mattered to her. She didn't want to go through her whole life not knowing . . .

"I'm going," she said, all the thoughts and events of the last few days crystallizing in that instant. "And I'm going right now."

Iowa wasn't so far away. If she had a car, she could be there in four hours. She glanced at the clock. If she left now, she could even be there before dark.

Just to see it one time. Just to touch it . . .

I'll take a bus. There have to be buses that go there.

In the library next door were the phone book and a big empty table to lay it on. Melanie hurried in and found the number for the major bus line, then reached for the phone at the edge of the table.

"Do you have a bus that goes to Iowa?" she asked the moment her call was answered.

"You going somewhere in particular?" a young-sounding guy asked with obvious amusement. "Or will any place in Iowa do?"

Melanie told him the name of the town, fidgeting impatiently with the phone cord.

"Leaving from?"

"Clearwater Crossing."

He chuckled. "Nothing leaves from Clearwater Crossing. The nearest bus depot is . . . Mapleton." He sounded as if he were reading it off a chart somewhere. "Do you want to leave from Mapleton?"

"I guess," she replied, wondering how she was going to get there.

"Okay. If you take the eight-fifteen into St. Louis tomorrow, you can transfer there. There are a few stops on the way, so let's see . . . that arrives in St. Louis at one-forty-five."

"A *few* stops?" Melanie cried.

"Then there's a little layover. Let's see. Looks like you need the three-twenty into Des Moines—that'd be the closest."

"Des Moines! That's not close at all. Besides, I want to leave today."

"Well . . . I could put you on a four-fifty into St. Louis. You could stay the night there, then in the morning—"

"No, you don't understand. I want to go and come back all in one day—today."

The reservations clerk laughed. "I'm only telling you what's possible. We don't make that trip direct—nobody does. Although it might be that Trailblazer goes into Ottumwa. . . . That'd be a little closer, but you'd have to—"

"Never mind." Melanie cut him off. "Thanks anyway." She hung up quickly and rubbed her aching temples.

The bus was a bad idea. That much was clear. Even if she found a better schedule, the stations weren't near enough to her origin or destination, and with all the stops and layovers the trip would take too long. She'd have to stay overnight some-where, which meant she'd have to tell her dad.

No. Totally unacceptable.

If only she were old enough to drive! She needed a faster, more direct way to travel. A *taxi?* Not at what they charged per mile.

Jesse. The answer came to her even as she tried to ignore it. She didn't want to go to Iowa with Jesse. The trip was too long. Jesse was too conceited, too annoying. . . .

Jesse's your only hope. The only other person she could even imagine asking was Peter, and Peter was at Rabbit Ridge. Besides, Jesse was more likely to say yes. He'd already told her that his brothers were flying to California to see his mother over the holidays and that his father wouldn't let him go. As disgusted as he'd been about that, he might just be in the mood for a little road trip. Quickly, before she could talk herself out of it, Melanie looked up his number and called him. Luckily, he was home.

"You want to go *where?*" Jesse said disbelievingly. "*Iowa?* What for?"

"For the day. I already told you that." As far as she was concerned, it was all he needed to know.

"I'm not just joyriding up to Iowa without some kind of reason," he said stubbornly. "If you can even call that joyriding. Besides, it's Christmas Eve tomorrow."

"So what? We'll be back before then."

"What are . . . you mean you want to leave *today*? You've got to be kidding me! It's already noon."

"It only takes about four—"

"Be serious, Mel. First I have to get some maps—not to mention permission. And I'm not driving home in the snow in the middle of the night on roads I've never seen."

"Don't call me Mel," she warned, momentarily forgetting to keep her voice sweet.

Jesse only laughed. "If I'm going to be your chauffeur, I guess I'll call you whatever I want."

"Try it. Then wait and hear what I call you."

"Temper, temper!" Jesse chided. He loved having the upper hand. "Now *why* are we going to Iowa?"

"If you drive me, I guess you'll find out. Otherwise, you can die wondering."

"Ooh, a mystery. All right. Unless I call back and say different, I'll pick you up at six tomorrow morning. But we're starting for home at two at the latest."

"Fine."

"That's all? Fine?"

He wants gratitude, she realized. *Ha! At this rate, he'll be lucky if I don't kill him.*

If there was any other way . . . But there wasn't.

"I mean, thanks a lot," she forced out somehow.

"Okay, see ya then."

Melanie hung up and wandered from the library

127

back to her room, tempted to call the whole thing off. She wasn't even sure what she thought going to Iowa would accomplish. But going with Jesse was almost certain to make her sorry she'd ever left home.

Maybe I should *call it off*, she thought, sitting down on the edge of her bed. The depression her body made caused something shiny to roll toward her: the angel ornament. She picked it up and held it to the light, examining the perfect, rainbow-hued bristles of the tiny paintbrush. Shaking off another of those strange sudden chills, she closed her hand gently around the thin glass.

No, I'm going. I'm definitely going.

"Why can't we?" Jason demanded. "You promised!"

Peter grimaced, then took a deep breath. He was trying to be understanding, but Jason's relentless whining and sulking were seriously trying his patience. The little boy's mittened fists were on his hips, and his usually milk white cheeks were as red as his hat as they faced off in the snow.

"I told you why—it's too late. By the time we got out to the hill with the sleds it would be dark." Peter glanced at the boys' cabin door, imagining how warm it would be inside. All the other kids had accepted his explanation as perfect sense and run in to beg for a snack before dinner. Only Jason wanted to argue.

128

"I could still go down one time. One time, Peter."

"Tomorrow. We'll get up and do it first thing."

"There probably won't even be snow tomorrow!" Jason shouted, his voice rising to a shriek. "Yesterday it melted. And tomorrow we're leaving early—there won't be any time!"

"There'll be plenty of time, and plenty of snow." The flakes had begun falling only an hour before, but it was so late in the day and they'd been coming down so steadily that Peter was sure he was right. "We'll get up early and go first thing—and you'll have the very first run."

"You always say that!" Jason howled. "You're a big liar!"

"Listen, Jason, it's not nice—"

"Don't talk to me!" Before Peter could say another word, Jason turned and ran into the cabin, slamming the door behind him.

Peter counted slowly to ten, then followed Jason's waffled bootprints through the snow. As he walked, he tried to remember every wise thing his parents had ever said to him when he was a little boy. Nothing appropriate came to mind. The problem was, he didn't even know what was bothering Jason. Not exactly.

Maybe I ought to get Dad to talk to him.

It couldn't hurt. Besides, he didn't have any other ideas.

But when he opened the cabin door, the angry

little towhead was nowhere to be seen. The rest of the boys were embroiled in a high-energy pillow fight in the living room, ganging up to pummel Ben. Chris egged them on from the relative safety of the dining nook while Mr. Altmann stirred a pot of spaghetti sauce on the stove.

Peter dodged the flying cushions and crossed quickly to his father. "Where's Jason?" he asked.

Mr. Altmann shook his head. "Came in here with a big chip on his shoulder and said he was going to bed." He pointed down the short hall with a dripping wooden spoon. "Took his sleeping bag in my room and shut the door."

"He can't just go to bed with no dinner!" Peter protested. "And I don't think he should go to sleep mad like that either. Besides, he hasn't washed up or brushed his teeth or—"

"Just leave him be, son," his father advised. "Give him a little peace. He'll come out when he smells the brownies your mom's baking for dessert."

Peter hesitated. For once he wasn't sure his father was correct. Jason had been so stubborn the last few days, Peter could easily imagine him starving himself to death just to make a point.

He took a deep breath and let it out slowly. He'd talk to Jason later. *Let's see if he comes out on his own, like Dad said.*

And in the meantime . . .

"I'm going to see if Mom needs any help with those brownies," he announced, heading for the exit.

"Yeah, right," Chris said. "Give Jenna a kiss for me, too."

I wish! Peter thought as he closed the door behind him. The way things had been going so far, he'd feel lucky if he even got to talk to her.

"Great," Nicole muttered, staring down at the bathroom scale Wednesday night. "That's just super."

She'd gained a pound over the last five days.

"It's all this sitting on my butt in Bible class," she complained to the four walls. "Mom promised I'd get *something* out of it."

The thing was, even as she said it, she knew she didn't really mean it. Something weird had happened on Monday, when big-mouthed Heather had spilled Nicole's deepest secret to a room full of total strangers: A few of the girls had actually come to her aid. Not to say she was right, but at least to say they understood. Even Greg had seemed supportive. Despite Heather's obvious intentions, he'd gone on with his little homily without embarrassing Nicole any further. And Nicole had taken care of Heather—there wouldn't be any more mouthing off from her.

Still . . . Greg's message had hit closer to home than Nicole liked to admit. She'd already known that her priorities weren't always good. She'd *tried* to change. But maybe lately she hadn't been trying as hard as she could have.

In the quiet of her bathroom, Nicole closed her eyes and took a deep breath. *It's just a pound,* she told herself. *It's neither bad nor good. It doesn't matter either way.*

She stepped resolutely off the scale, but the moment her foot touched the tile she snapped out of her trance and leapt back on.

A whole pound!

With an effort, she forced herself off again and went to her room to get ready for bed. *Jesse said you were too skinny anyway,* she remembered as she pulled on a loose flannel nightgown. Not that she'd believed him. If Jesse was right, all the fashion magazines were wrong—and just how likely was that?

She climbed heavily into bed. *Those magazines follow trends for the entire country. They have to know more than some guy in a backwoods like Clearwater Crossing.*

Even so, she had to admit she was tired of dieting. And she was thin now—as thin as she'd wanted to be.

I did my part, she thought, a little bitterly. But what had her struggle gotten her? Not Jesse, not the U.S. Girls title . . . not a darn thing. Her sacrifice hadn't brought her any of the things she'd dreamed of.

Maybe it was time to reevaluate.

Dear God, she prayed impulsively as her head touched her pillow, *if I'm completely blowing it here, could you please send me some type of sign?*

"I can't believe it's already our last night," Peter said. "Camp went by so fast."

His breath was visible even in the unlit interior of the bus, where Jenna had hoped the air might be warmer. The Junior Explorers were all in bed, so she and Peter couldn't talk in the cabins. From where they sat, Jenna could see that both living room windows were darkened, and only two little porch lights and the moon illuminated the blanket of snow between the buildings and the bus.

"If it means I get to sleep in a bed tonight, I'll believe anything you say," Jenna replied. "It's Maura's turn on the floor with the girls."

"Yeah. Chris has floor duty too."

Peter smiled, a flash of white teeth in the darkness, and Jenna felt her own lips curl in answer. She and Peter had barely been alone together the whole trip. They'd seen each other, of course, but he was always busy leading some sort of activity, or she was helping one of the girls take off five layers of clothing to use the bathroom. On top of that, the boys and girls were segregated five times a day, for three meals and two snacks, because there wasn't room for them all in either cabin. When Peter had come over to try to talk to her earlier that night, the girls had been taking their baths, one at a time in the little bathroom, and Jenna had been so hard pressed to keep a soaked and squirming Priscilla beneath the blow-dryer that they'd barely managed to exchange hellos.

Jenna sighed. "Winter camp is a lot harder than summer camp."

"Yeah. I never thought it would be, but you're right. Even with all the junk we brought, I'm always sure the kids must be freezing. I've probably spent eight hours just looking for lost hats and gloves."

"It makes you miss summer at the river," Jenna said nostalgically. "Running barefoot everywhere, swimming instead of showering, eating corn on the cob and watermelon in the outdoor dining hall . . ."

"Swatting mosquitoes as big as your fist."

"Okay. So chalk one up for winter camp."

Peter laughed. "I'd do this again, I'd just do it a little differently."

"Differently how?"

Peter dragged a fingertip through the condensation on the bus window beside him. "I'd try to find three cabins, for one thing, and set one up as the main kitchen and dining hall. It would be nicer if everyone could eat together, plus we could use those tables for crafts and games. Besides, with two extra bedrooms we could invite more people—like maybe some more of Eight Prime."

"You're still wishing Jesse had come, aren't you?"

He nodded. "More than ever. You've seen how Jason's been acting this trip—I don't know what to do with him."

"Jesse would know even less. You've spent more time around kids than he has."

"True. But I don't think Jason would be acting this way if Jesse were here." Peter shook his head. "He never did come out to dinner. When I finally went in to talk to him, he was sound asleep, still frowning. I wanted to wake him up, but my dad and Chris said to let him sleep." He sighed. "I have to admit, I didn't argue."

"Well, tomorrow he'll probably get up and go sledding and be just fine. And even if he's in a snit again, at least it's only for half a day. Tomorrow is Christmas Eve!"

Peter smiled. "I can't wait to see David."

"And go to the midnight service at church."

"Are you singing?"

"Mm-hmm." Jenna pulled her jacket tighter around her and looked hopefully toward the dashboard. "Brrr! I don't suppose we could turn on the heater?"

"Not without running the engine, and Chris has the keys. We'd probably better be going in anyway."

135

Jenna nodded. Neither of them moved.

"So when are we going to open our Christmas presents?" Peter asked. "Do you want to get together before church?"

"Uh, okay." She and Peter always exchanged their gifts on Christmas Eve, but she'd kind of been hoping to change that tradition this year, to give herself more time to find his present.

"I can't wait! I've had yours for almost two weeks, and I've been aching to give it to you ever since I bought it."

"Really?" she said with a weak smile. She had finally decided on a ski sweater for Peter. It wasn't very personal, but she'd noticed he could use a new one. Besides, everything else she'd thought of was either too dumb, or too expensive, or fatally flawed in some other way.

"Yeah. After we get home tomorrow, I want to spend some time with David. Then we'll be having dinner. Do you want to get together around eight?"

"Let me see . . . ," Jenna said slowly, calculating frantically. She'd have to go home before she went to the mall. Mary Beth would be there, so she'd have to at least say hello. Then she'd have to beg for a car, fight the last-minute crowds at the stores, pray she found something that she could afford, and hurry home for dinner. After dinner, she'd have to wrap Peter's sweater, wash her hair, and make herself halfway presentable for singing in choir. And that was just the stuff she knew about—her parents were sure to have more. Eight o'clock was cutting it too close.

"I think I'm going to be pretty busy. And you want to spend time with David. Why don't you just pick me up an hour early for church?" she suggested. "We can open our gifts then."

"All right. If you're sure your parents won't mind your riding to church with me instead of them."

"They won't," Jenna said hurriedly, unwilling to even consider the possibility that they might. The day already promised almost too much stress to handle. She was glad she'd at least decided on a gift to buy. She'd be running around like a maniac, but it was a relief to have a plan.

She stood up in the aisle. "Everything will be fine," she said, as much for her own benefit as Peter's.

Eleven

Peter woke up early on the last morning of winter camp. He lay still a moment, listening to the quiet, then slipped silently out of bed. Ben was snoring away in the other twin bed as Peter let himself into the hall, and the sound of heavy breathing came through the partially open door of his father's room too. Peter peered through the crack and made out the dark silhouettes of Jason's lumpy sleeping bag against the far wall and Mr. Altmann in bed.

In the living room, the other four boys were sleeping too, alongside Chris. Peter picked his way carefully around them to the living room window and drew back one edge of the insulated drapes.

He nearly gasped at the sight that met his eyes. *Oh, wow. The snow must have fallen all night.*

Outside the door was an unmarked carpet of white as deep as the front doorstep. Every tree dripped snow like vanilla icing. And the first rays of sun were breaking over the horizon, making the whole world sparkle.

Peter checked his watch, torn. He'd been looking forward to getting back home early that day and seeing his brother, but this was the kind of snow everyone had been hoping for. He'd have a battle on his hands trying to get the kids to leave at noon.

Which is why we should get started now, he thought, even though it was a good half hour earlier than he'd planned to wake them. *It's going to take time to get everyone dressed and fed, and I know Jason'll start whining about sledding the second he peeks outside. If we get started now, maybe we'll have less arguing later.*

He could hope so, anyway.

With a quick, decisive yank on the cord, Peter pulled the curtains open wide. "Rise and shine!" he hollered. "Wait till you see this snow!"

The kids bolted up out of their sleeping bags and crowded around the window.

"Cool!" Danny cried. "Me and Jason get the first turns on the sleds, don't forget!"

"Not likely," Chris muttered, rolling eyes glazed with sleep. He ran a hand through his spiky brown hair as he shuffled to the window. "Wow."

Soon all the kids were chattering excitedly as they hurried to put on their snow clothes. Danny and Elton wanted to sled right away, while Leo and Lars made plans to pelt the girls with snowballs first. Ben stumbled out of the bedroom and immediately reminded them all that he hadn't had a chance to ride a sled yet either. And last came Mr. Altmann, rubbing a chin thick with three-day-old stubble and looking as though he wouldn't have minded a couple more years in the sack.

"What time is it?" he asked. "And where's your mother with the coffee?"

"I woke everyone up a little early," Peter explained. "Look at all that snow!"

Mr. Altmann nodded, taking in the sight. "Where's Jason?"

"What . . . Well . . . Isn't he with you?"

"His sleeping bag is empty. I thought he was out here."

"The bathroom," Chris said quickly, before anyone could panic. But the bathroom door was standing wide open and nobody was inside.

"Jason?" Peter called nervously.

"Jason!" Ben bellowed at the top of his lungs.

"Calm down," Mr. Altmann said sharply. "He probably just went over to visit the girls."

"I'll go check," Peter said, grabbing his parka off a hook by the door and pulling it on over his pajamas. Stuffing his feet into his boots, he yanked the cabin door open, barely noticing the blast of frigid air that attacked his face. The snow he had thought so pretty just a minute before crested the tops of his boots and chilled his legs as he ran through it to the girls' front door. Stumbling on the stair, he grabbed their doorknob.

Locked. If the girls were up, they would have unlocked it.

"Hey!" he called, jiggling it frantically. "Hey, is Jason in there?" But he already knew he wasn't—not if the door was locked.

He glanced nervously over his shoulder at the boys' cabin, praying his dad and Chris had already found him.

Hey, maybe he's hiding under the bed! he thought, starting to jog back the way he'd just come. *That's exactly the type of prank Jason used to pull. He's under that double bed right now, laughing his head off about how—*

Peter stopped short. *Oh, no.*

One of the sleds was missing. Chris had left them both on the small wooden deck in back, and now there was only one.

The girls' front door opened.

"Peter? What's going on?" Maura's sleepy voice called. "Why would Jason be in here?"

Peter was too afraid to answer as he ran to the back of the boys' cabin. Small, waffled bootprints led from the back door down the stairs to the ground, but only a few feet from the cabin they began to lose definition. The slight wind that had started blowing had already partly filled them, and perhaps more snow had fallen too. Judging by their deteriorated condition, it had to have been dark when Jason left, and Peter had no doubt at all now where he had gone. The question was, was he okay?

He could be lost. He could be frozen, or hurt, or . . .

"Chris!" Peter shouted, weak with fear. "We have to go find Jason!"

Jesse pulled up to the intersection at the edge of town. "Okay, Melanie, enough with the cloak-and-dagger routine. I'm not getting on the freeway until you tell me where we're going."

As much as she didn't want him to know, Melanie knew she'd have to tell him eventually. She named her destination without meeting his eyes.

"We're going to a *cemetery*?" Jesse exclaimed disbelievingly. "For Pete's sake, Melanie, it's snowing!"

"It'll do that here in December," she said, sinking stubbornly into his black leather seat and crossing her arms across her chest, as if daring him to try to remove her. "Welcome to the Midwest."

He had shown up thirty minutes early, catching her completely unprepared. She'd been dressed, but she hadn't eaten, and she was still trying to stuff her backpack for the trip: money, keys, hat, gloves, an extra sweater . . . She'd been about to put in the funeral announcement with its map to the cemetery when she'd hear his knock on the door. Grabbing everything, she'd flown down the stairs, anxious to keep him from waking her father.

"What are you doing here so early?" she'd whispered. "I'm not ready."

"You look ready to me."

She'd glared at him in reply, then let him into the entryway. "Wait here."

Running into the kitchen, she'd grabbed a pad and pen off the breakfast bar. She hadn't told her father she was leaving, but she'd planned to write him a note. She'd also planned to have a few quiet minutes to figure out what to say. She'd held the pen over the paper a minute, then doodled curlicues along the edge. Knowing that Jesse was standing by the door, waiting, had made her too nervous to think.

"So, are we leaving or what?" Jesse had suddenly asked behind her. "Because if we aren't I've got better things—"

"I told you to wait by the door!" she'd whispered, spinning around and gesturing frantically for him to keep his voice down.

Abandoning the paper and pen where they were, she'd ushered Jesse quickly out of the kitchen. Her father would just have to see her when she got back, the way he did the rest of the time. The only reason she'd planned to leave him a note in the first place was because it was Christmas Eve.

Forget about it, she'd advised herself as she'd walked out the door with Jesse and down to his waiting car. *By noon, he'll be too drunk to even notice you're missing.*

"We're going to be fighting the weather the whole way," Jesse whined now. "And for what? If the ground's all covered with snow you won't even be able to find her grave."

"It's barely snowing, Jesse. Besides, that's what headstones are for."

"Huh? Oh. In California, they usually put the markers flat to the grass. It's supposed to make us think we're in a park or something."

Melanie tried to smile as if interested, but she was sick of hearing about California. She wished Jesse would find some other subject—or, better yet, stop talking altogether.

By the end of the first hour on the road, she wished it more than ever. She'd had no idea what an eternity four hours could be when a person was trapped in a car with a self-centered peacock like Jesse. He'd been building himself up the entire drive.

And finally Melanie could no longer resist the temptation to tear him back down. He was bragging about being the MVP in the Red River game when he gave her an opening too good to pass up.

"Everything was just so smooth that night, you know?" he gloated. "My catching, my running. Everything clicked. I was just so . . . smooth."

"Yeah. Like the way you handled Vanessa at the victory party. That was *real* smooth. In case you care, by the way, she's still not speaking to me."

Jesse shrugged. "Then I did you a favor."

"She's my squad captain, Jesse! Before you pulled

144

your little date-'em-and-dump-'em act, you might have taken ten seconds to consider that I'll be cheering with her for the rest of the year. But no, you just walked away and left me stuck with your mess."

Jesse's blue eyes narrowed moodily. "You're exaggerating."

"And you're a selfish flirt who's going to run through half the girls in Clearwater Crossing—the half that's stupid enough to go out with you."

"That shows how much you know about girls. The more you dump, the more who get in line."

Melanie took a deep breath. "How sad that you believe that," she said disdainfully.

"I *know* that."

"Even sadder."

They glared at each other a moment.

"You know what? Don't take it out on me because your mom died, Melanie. I'm not exactly the world's happiest camper right now myself."

"Oh, you have it so tough. Just because you didn't get to fly out to California—"

"My mom might as well be dead, as often as I get to see her."

Melanie stared, unable to believe even Jesse capable of such a heartless comparison. "You're an idiot," she told him. "Not only is that just about the stupidest thing I ever heard, you don't even know it."

"I *must* be an idiot," he shot back, "to be driving

your ungrateful butt anywhere. I don't know why I bother with you."

"Then turn the car around."

"Fine."

"Fine."

But he didn't.

"I can't believe this class is already over," Brenda said, helping herself to an iced sugar cookie from the refreshments table.

Greg was playing his guitar on the other side of the room, and the rest of the Teen Extreme students milled around at their farewell party, talking, singing along, or filling up on the assortment of holiday goodies they'd all brought to share with the group. "Except for Guy's little holier-than-thou moments, it went really fast."

"It did," Nicole agreed, magnanimous in her relief. There had been times she'd been sure it would never end, and Bible class still wasn't what she'd have *chosen* to do with her vacation. But in the end . . . well, it hadn't been all that bad. Besides, why hold a grudge when tomorrow was Christmas—not to mention the first of ten glorious days of vacation fun with Courtney?

Her friend had had a fit when she'd first found out about Teen Extreme, but once she'd learned that Guy was in it too, amusement had gotten the upper hand. Since then, Courtney had called every night for "progress reports"—her term for rubbing it in. Yes, Nicole was glad the class was over.

"Whoops. Here comes Guy, looking serious." Brenda made a sour face. "I just remembered, I need to be anywhere else."

She was off in a flash, leaving Nicole to wonder once again if Brenda knew what had happpened between her and Guy—Nicole had never felt brave enough to ask her. Nicole considered trying to dodge off somewhere herself, but it was too late. Guy was not only looking right at her, she seemed to be the reason he was making the trip.

He stopped a couple of feet away. They faced each other uncertainly, Nicole with her back to the refreshments, Guy shifting nervously from foot to foot. "Well . . . so . . . I just wanted to say goodbye," he said stiffly. "I'm glad you were part of our group."

Nicole felt her eyebrows shoot up. She forced them back down and worked to make her face expressionless. "Thank you," she said, more coolly than she'd intended. "I mean, it was, uh, interesting."

Guy's gaze had fastened on the diet soda in her hand. Nicole self-consciously shifted the label away from him.

"You know, you're really very thin," he said quietly. "It was the first thing I noticed about you."

"Thank you," she said again.

"It's just a fact. I didn't mean it as a compliment."

Guy's worried eyes searched hers. On an impulse, Nicole reached behind her, grabbed a gooey chocolate cookie, and took a big bite. Her inquisitor relaxed noticeably.

"Don't believe everything you hear from Heather," she advised him when she could swallow.

He laughed. "Ditto for Brenda."

He had a nice, genuine laugh. Nicole had noticed it before but hadn't let herself admit it.

"Why?" she teased, warming to him a little. "What do you think she told me?"

"I wouldn't even want to guess."

Nicole finished off her cookie and picked up a candy cane. She'd have to skip lunch later, but it was a small price to pay to set the record straight. "You know how sisters are," she said breezily. "Although *you* could have done a lot worse. Wanna trade me and find out?"

Guy shook his head. "You don't really mean that. Heather's a great kid."

Of course he'd think so—they're practically peas in a pod. Brenda and I are much more alike.

"I guess she's bearable in small doses," Nicole allowed.

Guy chuckled again, and his smile reached up into his eyes. He almost seemed like a different person now than the boy she'd gone on that blind date with. Not that he was suddenly her type or anything—far from it—but he didn't seem quite so bad anymore either.

"Hey, Guy!" Greg called suddenly. "How about helping me out over here?"

"Oops. I promised I'd spell him on the guitar," Guy told her, nodding acknowledgment to Greg. "I'd better go."

"You play guitar?"

He shrugged. "I try."

Nicole glanced toward the door. "I was getting ready to leave anyway. I guess I'll see you around." She knew she never would.

"All right. See you." He brought one hand up in a half wave before he headed off to play "Jingle Bells" or "Kumbaya" or whatever it was he knew.

For a moment she actually considered hanging around until the end of the party to see if she could entice him into asking her out. He seemed to be taking her more seriously now. If she played her cards right, it wasn't inconceivable he'd be interested. Or maybe she'd even ask him. What a relief it would be to dump him afterward and finally make things even.

She sighed. For some reason she just didn't think she'd enjoy it as much anymore.

Oh, what the heck, she thought generously, deciding to let it go. *It's Christmas Eve. Put the past behind you and move on.*

Guy was just sitting down, adjusting the guitar strap over his shoulder. Nicole felt incredibly big-hearted and mature as she waved good-bye to him from across the room and walked out of his life forever.

Twelve

Don't panic. Don't panic, Jenna told herself over and over again. The words were a chant keeping time to her steps as she trudged through the snowy woods. She'd been out searching for Jason for hours, along with nearly everyone else. Only Mrs. Altmann had stayed behind at the cabins, to supervise the ten remaining Junior Explorers.

When Jason had first been discovered missing, Peter and Chris had gone out to search alone. They'd hurried to the sled hill while everyone else had tried to pretend everything was normal. Ben and Mr. Altmann had gotten the boys dressed and fed, while Jenna, Maura, and Mrs. Altmann had taken care of the girls. But when breakfast had ended and Chris and Peter hadn't returned, when the dishes had been washed up, when Mrs. Altmann began packing boxes with the pots and pans she wouldn't need again and Chris and Peter *still* hadn't returned, the fear Jenna had been pushing to the back of her mind all morning had settled into her gut like lead.

151

And then the snow had started again, blunting the edges of the footprints outside and filling every depression.

At last Peter and Chris had come jogging back into sight—alone.

"He's not at the hill," Peter had explained, his eyes wild with worry. "He *was* there. We found some tracks. But now . . . the snow . . ." His cheeks had been red and his chest had heaved with exertion. His bangs had dripped moisture where they'd stuck out under his knit cap.

"We need more people," Chris had concluded as Mrs. Altmann had come running to stuff their coat pockets with granola bars, cheese, and chocolate to make up for the breakfast they'd missed. "We've got to send everyone out in different directions to cover more area."

"No one's running around in the woods solo— not in this weather," Mr. Altmann had contradicted him. "We'll work in pairs. Chris, you take Maura. Jenna, go with Peter. Ben and I will make up the third."

But that had been hours before, and even as cold and uncomfortable as they were, the morning had slipped swiftly away as they'd searched. Jenna's face and feet were freezing now, her stomach rumbled with hunger, and her legs felt like rubber from forcing them through the snow. And still there was no sign of Jason. Despite Mr. Altmann's admonitions that no one work alone, she and Peter had taken to making small sweeps in opposite directions to cover more ground, meeting back up near where they had started.

"Jason!" she called, her throat raw from shouting.

"Jason!" Peter's faint echo floated back to her through the woods.

A gust of wind blew snow into her face. She blinked the flakes out of her lashes and pulled her scarf over her nose. "Jason!"

"It's no use," Peter said when they met again. "I haven't seen a thing, have you?"

Jenna shook her head. "I can barely see where I'm going. And it's so cold, Peter."

"Are you okay?" he asked, his concern temporarily changing focus.

"I'm fine. It's just that . . ." She shook her head, unwilling to say any of the frightening things she was thinking.

"We have to get more help. A real search-and-rescue team would have dogs, and radios, and I don't know what."

A whistle drifted to them faintly through the falling snow: Mr. Altmann's signal to meet on the trail.

Peter's head jerked up. "Thank God! Maybe they found him!"

But back on the trail, the news was dismal.

"We're going to have to call the rangers," Mr.

Altmann said when everyone had gathered. "And as much as I hate to upset her, we'd better call Mrs. Brown."

He handed Peter the cellular phone they'd brought on the trip. "Peter, you and Jenna go back to the cabins. Make sure Jason hasn't shown up there on his own. If he hasn't, start making calls."

Peter immediately turned to Jenna and pressed the phone into her gloved hands. "It's my fault he's lost in the first place," he said urgently. "I can't quit looking while I know he's still out here. Can you go back without me?"

She nodded, sure she could find her way. But Mr. Altmann wouldn't hear of it. "We're not splitting up the pairs, Peter. If anything, you and Chris should both be going in, since you've been out here the longest."

"Not me," Chris said immediately. "Jason's my responsibility too, don't forget."

"Let's not start talking about blame and responsibility," Mr. Altmann said, looking back and forth from Peter to Chris. "If we're going to find Jason, we need to work as a team."

"Fine. But with all due respect, sir, I'm not going back," Chris said stubbornly.

Mr. Altmann's face clouded at the challenge.

Jenna jumped into the conversation. "Mr. Altmann's right. We don't have time to fight." She managed to catch Ben's eye, sending him a desperate look.

"I'll go!" he volunteered loudly, understanding her unspoken message. "Let *me* walk back with Jenna."

Mr. Altmann looked uncertain. "All right, then," he said finally. "And Peter can team with me. Same signals as before. Ben, you and Jenna be sure to put on dry clothes before you come back out here."

"I wish we had two cell phones," Jenna said. "Then if he was at the cabins we could call you and you could come in quicker."

"I know. We'll just have to make the best of it."

Jenna tucked the cell phone carefully inside her down parka. Then she and Ben took off down the trail.

Please, God, she prayed as they hurried toward the cabins. *Please let Jason be there, and please let him be all right.*

She glanced back over her shoulder at Peter, already nearly swallowed up by the falling snow, and felt a different kind of fear.

And please keep them safe too.

"What do you mean, you lost the map?" Jesse asked, his voice barely under control.

"Which word didn't you understand?" Melanie

snapped, digging madly through her backpack. "I, lost, the, map."

"How could you—"

"If you hadn't shown up so early, before I was even ready to—"

"Oh, so now it's *my* fault we're lost in Nowheresville, Iowa, without a map, in the middle of a blizzard."

"You call this a blizzard?" she asked scornfully. "You wouldn't know a blizzard if somebody drew you a nice colored picture."

"Yeah? Well, here's a picture: You've got five minutes to figure out where this place is, or I'm turning my car around."

"I'm not going home now, Jesse."

"Fine by me. I'll be more than happy to let you out right here."

Melanie squeezed the fabric of her backpack with both hands and closed her mouth tight against all the possible retorts that came to mind. She knew she'd had the funeral card in her hand when Jesse had knocked—she must have left it on her bed when she'd run down to answer the door.

"Just let me see your map," she said, reaching for it. "I'm sure I can find the cemetery on there."

"You're kidding me, right? This is a *road* map, Melanie. This whole town barely even registers as a blip."

"Well, if it's such a little blip, then we can't be

all that lost, now can we? We could probably drive around until—"

"I'm not just driving at random in this crappy weather in this Podunk little town—"

"For crying out loud, Jesse, cut me some slack! I messed up, all right? Is that what you want me to say?" She felt tears pooling in her eyes and fought to keep them back. "Just . . . stop at a gas station, okay? Stop anywhere. I'll find out where we are."

He took the first right, into a restaurant parking lot, and she climbed out of the car without a word. A light snow was falling, but there wasn't much on the ground. Melanie hurried into the brightly lit restaurant, where the only other person in sight was a waitress drinking coffee at the counter. She turned her head at the sound of the opening door.

"You ain't here to eat, are ya?" she guessed, taking in Melanie's troubled expression. "At this rate, I have half a mind to close the place up and call it Christmas early."

"Amen," a disembodied voice answered from the kitchen.

Melanie explained her situation and a minute later returned to Jesse's idling car with a penciled map drawn on a napkin. She handed it over without comment, heaving a sign of relief when he silently backed up the car and drove out of the parking lot.

They didn't speak all the way to the cemetery.

Their silence continued even when he drove through the open iron gates. Melanie tensed up, waiting for the inevitable questions about which way to go and where to park, but Jesse had finally seemed to grasp that she didn't know any more than he did. He drove to a place near the center of the sprawling burial ground, stopped the car, and turned off the engine.

Quickly, before he could open his mouth, Melanie pushed her door open and jumped out. A cutting wind blew, and the temperature seemed lower than it had at the restaurant, but she walked determinedly away from the BMW, shoving her hands deep into her pockets. In her haste, she'd forgotten her gloves, but there was no way she was going back for them now and risk having Jesse try to accompany her. *Let him wait in his precious car.*

The cemetery was old and haphazard, with family plots incorporating both old and new graves, and rows of markers that didn't run straight. Some of the older limestone monuments were so weathered the engraving was nearly gone, while only a few feet away a headstone of imposing black granite would have letters as sharp as broken glass. Melanie wandered from plot to plot, her booted feet marring the otherwise undisturbed mantle of snow.

At last she found it, half a football field in front of Jesse's car and over to the right. The stone was a simple gray rectangle with a highly polished face and coarsely hewn back and sides. It fit, somehow. Melanie could imagine her mother picking it out for herself. *Maybe she did*, she realized uneasily—just one more thing Melanie didn't know.

Almost involuntarily her bare right hand floated out of her pocket and reached for the marker's uneven top. Her fingers touched stone so cold it seemed to suck the warmth right out of them. She recoiled, then tried again, tracing the deeply etched letters of her mother's name:

TRISTYN ALLEN ANDREWS

Melanie's hand was a clumsy mitt, already numb from the cold. She dropped it to her side, uncertain what to do next.

She couldn't believe she was there. It didn't seem real, somehow, standing on that white carpet of snow, her mother's headstone a slightly lighter gray than the smothering sky overhead. She had expected to feel something big, had hoped for some sort of connection. But instead all she felt was stupid, and self-conscious, and hyperaware of Jesse's critical presence in the parked car somewhere behind her.

Dropping abruptly to her knees, she fumbled in her coat pocket and pulled out her secret package: the angel with the paintbrush. The red silk scarf she'd wound it in made a flash of crimson against the colorless landscape as she unwrapped the delicate ornament. The glass glimmered even under that dull sky, and for a moment Melanie hesitated. Then she scooped back the snow at the base of the headstone and laid the angel in the depression. The delicate face looked up at her serenely, perfect. Closing her eyes, Melanie pushed the snow back into place.

Lurching to her feet, she wheeled around blindly and walked back the way she had come until her eye caught another splash of red—Jesse's BMW. *No*, she thought. *I can't face Jesse. Not yet.* Altering direction abruptly, she headed for a small chapel she'd seen near the gate.

The door grated open on protesting hinges, and Melanie stepped hesitantly through the doorway. It was as cold inside as out. The dim daylight barely illuminated the stained-glass windows and the simple wooden cross at the front. The aisle was down the side, and there were only three small pews. Even to Melanie's inexperienced eyes it was clear that the chapel was a place to pray, not a place to hear a sermon. She sat in the third pew, the wood nearly as cold through her jeans as the stone outside had been.

She didn't know what she was doing there, either. She only knew she couldn't go back—not to the car, not to Clearwater Crossing. Not yet. To pass the time, she looked through the materials in the wooden pew pocket in front of her. There was a Bible, a book of prayers, and the type of short, eraserless pencil golfers used to keep score. The pencil had been deeply chewed, the Bible scribbled on. The pew itself was dusty. Melanie registered the information, but it didn't mean anything. Her heart felt as numb as her hands had been.

Does anyone ever really find comfort in a place like this? she wondered. But even as she asked the question, she knew they did. Peter and Jenna were living proof that comfort could be found in a church. *So what's wrong with me?*

The door squealed open again—Jesse. Determined not to speak to him, Melanie didn't acknowledge his presence even when he sat down beside her. But the longer he held his silence, the more her resistance wavered . . . and time dragged in that cold, cold room. Finally she blurted out the thing so heavy on her mind.

"Do you feel anything in here?"

"Like what?" he asked.

"I don't know. Like God."

He cringed a little, then shook his head. "I used to. In church, I mean. But lately I don't anymore. I don't know why."

"I never did," she said sadly. "I wanted to. I always wanted to. And today, especially, I wanted to feel *something* . . . something besides the cold . . ."

And then, like a bubble breaking up toward the

surface, the first sob rose out of her body, too quick to hide and too loud to stifle. She closed her eyes and cried, sitting upright on that hard bench, her bare fingers clutching the edge until her knuckles stiffened. A minute passed, an hour—time stood still while she wept. Then her aching left hand was covered by a large warm one and a protective arm slipped lightly across her shoulders.

She turned to Jesse, her eyes opening wide. They searched each other's faces. There was an unexpected trace of moisture in his lashes, a suspicious-looking track down one cheek . . . and all at once Melanie was in his arms, her face pressed into his jacket.

"Oh, Jesse," she cried. "Oh, God. What am I doing here?"

Miguel's eyes were even more intense than usual as he trained them on the snowy road passing beneath his tires. "I thought we'd be there by now. Do you think we could have passed it?"

"No," Leah said immediately. "No way." She'd been keeping a sharp lookout for the cabins, and even assuming she could have overlooked them somehow, there wasn't a chance she'd have missed that powder blue bus. "They must be up ahead."

She strained forward to better see out the windshield. They had come as soon as Jenna had called them, but first they'd had to get dressed for the snow, and then Miguel had had to swing by to pick her up. An eternity had passed before they were actually on the road.

"I hope Jason is okay," Leah said, chewing at the corner of one unpolished thumbnail.

"He is," Miguel replied tensely. "Don't even think about it."

But she couldn't stop thinking about it. About all the horrible things that could happen to a six-year-old alone in the snow . . .

"There! There's the bus!" she cried. She pointed up ahead, but Miguel was already steering his car to the side of the road. She leaned across him to peer out his window, down to the cabins.

"There are a bunch of people down there," she reported as he stopped beside a few other cars and pickups. "And I think I see Jenna."

Jenna stood at the edge of a milling group out in front of the cabins. As Leah and Miguel rushed out of his car, she began walking away from them.

"Jenna!" Leah shouted, stumbling toward her through the snow. "Jenna, wait!"

Miguel passed Leah by. "Jenna!" he called in his deep voice.

Jenna turned around, her face drawn with exhaustion. Her cheeks and lips were chapped, her long hair full of snow and ice. Her eyes were still hopeful, though, as she hurried over to greet them. "You came!" she said, as if there'd been any chance they wouldn't.

"Of course we did," said Miguel. "What should we do? Is there a plan, or is everyone just setting out on their own?"

Jenna shook her head and pointed past the cabins up the trail, where the rest of the group was heading. "The rangers are organizing teams up there and giving everyone search areas. Nicole and her father came too, and some of my family just got here. Jason's mom, Peter's brother . . . I couldn't get hold of Melanie or Jesse, but I left messages on their answering machines."

She looked so frazzled that Leah put a comforting hand on her arm, pushing her own doubts aside for her friend. "Don't worry. I know we're going to find him."

"I hope so." Jenna's voice caught in her throat. She turned her face away, as if to hide impending tears.

Leah nudged Miguel in the ribs, pleading with her eyes for him to say something reassuring.

"We heard a bulletin on The Buzz driving up here," Miguel blurted out, naming the local radio station. "They said the rangers were searching for a kid lost in the snow, and they gave a number people can call if they want to help—especially people with dogs."

"Really?" Jenna looked at them again and, as Leah had suspected, her eyes were glassy with barely suppressed tears. "We have a couple of dogs already." She gestured up ahead again. "Come on, we'd better hurry. My dad and Caitlin are here. And my oldest sister, Mary Beth. She got back from college yesterday."

"You look so tired," Leah said. "Now that all these people are here, can't you take a rest?"

Jenna shook her head. "Peter and Chris are even more exhausted than I am and they haven't rested once. We're the ones who brought Jason up here. We're the ones who have to . . ."

Her voice broke again, and this time two big tears spilled over and rolled down her cheeks. "I'm sorry. I'm just so scared for him."

"We all are. But we're going to find him. How can we miss, with all this help? Come on, now, you have to think positive."

Jenna lifted her chin a little. "You're right. We have to have some faith."

"That's the spirit," Miguel said.

Leah and Miguel put their arms around Jenna, one on each side, and together the three of them hurried to join the search.

Thirteen

The digital clock on the dashboard was displaying 3:13 as Jesse's car reached the county line. Melanie read the numbers through half-closed eyes, then snapped upright in her seat and read them again. She'd been asleep for nearly three hours!

"Have a nice nap?" Jesse asked, with just a trace of his former sass.

"I . . . Why didn't you wake me up?" she demanded.

He shrugged. "I figured you were happier the way you were. Besides, it's not like you missed anything." He gestured through the windshield to the snow coming down outside. "White any way you look. There. You've already seen it all."

She relaxed a little and rubbed her tired eyes, hoping they weren't crusted with sleep and mascara. Not that she probably had any makeup left after the way she'd bawled on Jesse's jacket. Her cheeks flushed at the memory . . . Jesse's arms around her, his hands stroking her back and shoulders, his lips in her hair for the briefest of

166

moments—at least she was pretty sure they had been in her hair—and then his whispered words: "Come on. I'll take you home."

She glanced at him sideways now, embarrassed. At the time his comforting had seemed natural. The gentle way he'd guided her out to his car had seemed sweet. On the way home, he'd bought her lunch at a Taco Bell and not even flinched when she'd accidentally dripped taco sauce on his leather seat. There had been not one comment about the distance, the snow, the cold, California . . .

Still . . . she'd promised herself once that she'd never let Jesse get close to her. And she wasn't about to change such a sensible resolution simply because he'd managed to act human for the last four hours.

"How about some music?" she asked, reaching forward to turn on his radio before he could reply.

The local station was playing Christmas songs. Carols wouldn't have been Melanie's first choice, but at least music was better than talk. With very little news to report and no high-priced radio personalities to boast of, the station frequently used up time by making community service announcements. Everything from upcoming church suppers to garage sales got announced over its airwaves, a practice Jesse had commented on scornfully during the drive north that morning. By now, though, so late on Christmas Eve, Melanie suspected they were probably running a prerecorded tape.

The car was gliding peacefully down the road into town when "Oh Come, All Ye Faithful" was ineptly terminated short of the final note and a bumbling male announcer took the mike. "Okay! That was real nice, now wasn't it? We have just a few announcements here on this fine Christmas Eve. . . ."

Irritated by the interruption, Melanie reached reflexively for the dial, but the next words the dee-jay said stopped her hand in midair.

"The search-and-rescue team is still looking for that missing child up near Rabbit Ridge. They're spreading out now and calling for more volunteers. If you want to help, and especially if you have walkie-talkies, call 555-9834."

"Oh, no!" Melanie gasped, her throat tightening with panic. "It's Amy."

"You don't know that," Jesse said. "You don't even know it's one of the Junior Explorers."

"It is! That's where their cabins were." An awful dread gripped her at the thought of Amy lost in the snow, all alone with darkness coming. "Turn around, Jesse. Turn this car!"

He seemed to catch some of her fear as he cranked his wheel in the direction she pointed, almost losing control as his car slid through an icy curve.

"That way! Now that way!" Melanie shouted directions, more frantic with each passing moment. They were at least twenty-five minutes from the ridge, and the drive would take longer in such snowy weather. Her heart pounded as Jesse navigated the dangerous twists and turns of the slippery back roads she led him down. Jesse's eyes betrayed no nervousness, but a muscle jumped in his jaw as he wrestled with the wheel.

They didn't speak except to discuss directions. Only once Jesse said, "You can't be sure it's Amy."

"It's one of them, anyway. We have to help," Melanie replied tightly.

At last the powder blue bus came into view, its roof covered with snow. Three men with shovels and a blower were digging it out and keeping things clear for the cluster of cars and pickups parked nearby.

Jesse skidded to the edge of the makeshift lot, parked, and jumped out immediately. "Who's lost?" he called to the nearest man as Melanie struggled out the passenger door, pulling on her gloves. "Who's the kid?"

"Little boy. Jason something."

Melanie's legs almost failed her in her relief.

It's just as bad for Jason to be lost as Amy, she reminded herself hurriedly. *But . . .*

And then she saw Jesse's face. The strength that had returned to her with the news that Amy was safe seemed to have drained directly from him. Why had it never occurred to her during all that long ride that Jesse would be worried about one special kid too?

"Oh, Jesse, I'm so—" she started, but he cut her off abruptly.

"This is all my fault! I should have been here!" He zipped his parka up and jammed a hat over his short hair. "Jason wanted me here. Peter *asked* me to be here."

"You don't know if that would have made any difference." She was acutely aware of the sudden reversal of their roles as she put a tentative, comforting hand on his arm. "It's not your fault, Jesse. Besides, we're going to find him."

"We'd better," Jesse said grimly. "And he'd better be all right."

Two squatty cabins were set back from the road. Lights were on in both front windows, and through one of them Melanie could see the shadowed shapes of kids and adults. She longed to visit Amy, if only for a moment.

"Let's go down there," she said, pointing. "Someone inside can tell us how to help."

They started toward the buildings just as another car appeared, driving cautiously down the snowy road. They both turned their heads, and Melanie gasped. The car was her father's.

"You go on without me," she told Jesse nervously, wondering how her father could have found her. "I'll catch up in a minute."

Jesse nodded and trudged ahead, too impatient to be curious. Melanie watched as Mr. Andrews parked and climbed slowly out of the car.

Is he angry? Of course he is—he came to get you, didn't he?

She shifted anxiously from foot to foot as he made his way toward her. Then suddenly she realized that she hadn't seen him truly dressed for the snow since her mother had died. When the weather was bad, he simply stayed inside or, at most, threw on a coat for the run from the car to some building. The outdoor clothes he wore that afternoon were old and familiar, and as he walked toward her across the snow she was struck mostly by how large for him they'd become.

He'd shrunk.

"Dad, what are you doing here?" she asked.

He smiled. "Same as you, I imagine. I came to look for Jason."

"But . . ."

"Your friend Jenna left a message on our answering machine for you. When you didn't come home, and they still hadn't found him . . . well, I guess I just can't bear the thought of anyone losing someone they love. Especially a child."

She stared at him, wondering how many hidden messages were embedded in what he'd just said.

171

"How was Iowa?" he asked.

"What?" she exclaimed. "How did you know?"

He reached into his pocket and produced the funeral announcement. "I found this on the breakfast bar, along with the pen and paper for the note you didn't write. With clues like that, Sherlock Holmes could have retired."

Melanie took the card in a daze. *I must have carried it downstairs, then forgotten it in my rush to get Jesse out of the kitchen*, she realized.

"Did you find what you were looking for?" her father asked.

She shook her head with her eyes still on the card. The tears that suddenly filled them blurred the edges of the paper.

When she looked up again, he was gone—off to join a search party emerging from the cabin. Jesse was with them, and she thought she recognized Ben as well.

Melanie tucked the card into her jacket and wiped her face with her gloves. Then, taking a long, deep breath, she ran down the hill to catch up.

"You should go back and rest," Jesse told Peter brusquely. "You're only slowing me down."

"Then don't wait for me," Peter retorted, exhausted.

Ever since Jesse had shown up, he'd been trying to run the show. First he'd managed to mani-

172

pulate the groups so that he and Peter were together and Jenna was with Ben and Caitlin. Then he'd started inventing his own search plans, venturing into ravines and other dangerous areas the rangers had told the volunteers to avoid. "If Jason were anywhere easy, you guys would've found him by now," was the logic he'd used to justify his actions. And, feeling guilty and nearly desperate, Peter had given in.

Now Jesse looked half ready to take Peter up on his offer and ditch him. He began to turn his back, then stopped and shook his head. "If he's hurt when I find him, one of us might have to stay out here while the other one runs back to camp. You're just going to have to keep up."

Somehow Peter managed to keep from saying anything as he scrambled up out of the creek bottom behind Jesse, his hands and feet slipping on the snowy rocks until his muscles nearly gave out. As irritating as Jesse's attitude was, Peter knew where it came from: Jesse was as convinced it was his fault that Jason had run away that morning as Peter was that it was his own. Jesse had already said as much. And both of them were scared—too scared to admit it to each other. Almost too scared even to admit it to themselves. Every time Peter thought of Jason, he immediately envisioned an arm out of its socket, or a badly broken leg twisted impossibly beneath an unconscious body.

173

Or worse.

Peter caught his breath as another gush of adrenaline rocked through him, making his stomach churn. What if they didn't find him?

We will. That's all. He forced his slogging feet through the snow a little faster. He wanted to pray, but he'd already said every prayer he could think of.

He just couldn't believe this was happening—to Jason or to him. It didn't seem fair, somehow. Not after he'd tried so hard to be a good person. And that it should happen on Christmas Eve . . .

Suddenly God felt very far away.

"Okay, wait," Jesse said, stopping so abruptly that Peter slammed into his back. "We're going about this all wrong."

"Because?" Peter asked tightly, taking a step backward.

"Because walking these patterns takes too much time. It'll be dark in another half hour."

The truth of Jesse's words made Peter light-headed with fear. Nightfall was coming. If they hadn't found Jason by then . . .

"What do you think we ought to do?" he asked, and his voice sounded brittle in his ears.

"Jason wanted to go sledding, right? We ought to be looking on the highest hill there is, not down in these stupid ravines."

Peter managed not to point out that it had been Jesse's idea to search the creek bottoms in the first place. "We've triple-searched the best sledding hill in the area," he said, impatient to move again. "Chris and I went over the whole thing twice, and then they did it again with the dogs."

"Right. And you said he'd definitely been there with the sled. So where did he go? To a bigger hill, of course."

"There *is* no bigger hill," Peter argued. "I've told you and told you that that's the best—"

"He's a *kid*, Peter! Try to think like a kid for a minute. Geez. To kids, bigger is always better. You could have told him a *million* times that that was the best sled hill. If he knew there was a bigger one, he'd want to try it."

Peter opened his mouth to say Jason would have to be insane to wander off by himself to a hill he'd never tried, just because he thought it might be a little longer or a little faster than Peter's hill. In nearly the same instant, he knew that Jesse was right. That was exactly what Jason would do.

"There are lots of hills around here," he said, trying to control his panic. "He could have gone to any of them."

"He could have, but he wouldn't," Jesse insisted. "The *biggest* one, Peter. Which one is the biggest?"

"I don't even know, exactly. I'd have to get a map and—"

"Which one *looks* the biggest?" Jesse broke in impatiently. "For God's sake, Peter, use your head!"

Peter tried to calm down enough to remember which hills Jason might have seen on their various rambles through the woods, and which one might have appealed to him. They had never wandered more than a mile or so from the cabins, always planning their hikes to make large, irregular loops that ended where they'd started. The farthest they'd ever gone was Pine Hollow, and the hill down into the hollow wasn't nearly as steep as the one Jason had started out on that morning. Even if he'd climbed all the way to the top of the hollow . . .

"No, he wouldn't . . ." Peter began slowly.

"What?"

Peter's mind was racing. From the top of the ridge around the hollow, a person could see a long way. They had taken all the kids up there the first afternoon, when the ground had been mostly bare. Looking back toward the cabins from that vantage point, no peak had seemed higher. But looking the opposite way, down the rugged back of the ridge and far into the distance, the next set of hills had shimmered temptingly.

"Those hills have more snow than ours!" Jason had complained.

Chris had shaken his head. "It probably just looks that way because they're so far off. I guess maybe they could at the top, though. They are a little higher."

And there had been one hill, in particular. One

rough, rocky knob of a hill perched on top of a gentler slope . . .

"He wouldn't," Peter said again.

"He would!" Jesse insisted. "Stop wasting time—you *know* he would. Where is it?"

Peter stretched up a little taller and fixed his eyes off in the distance. From where they were, he couldn't even see where they'd be going. Setting out for that hill now, on their own, would break every rule the rangers had read them. On the other hand, going back to explain their theory would just mean more lost time. And every minute lost was a minute closer to darkness. . . .

Peter started to run. "Follow me!" he cried.

"I can't believe he's leaving," Jenna said, nearly frantic as she watched through the cabin window.

Outside in the falling twilight, Chris pulled the bus onto the road. The vehicle began toiling up the grade with all the Junior Explorers aboard. All but one.

"He'll be back," Caitlin said soothingly from beside her.

"It's better to get the kids home now, before it gets dark," Ben said from her other side. "Besides, with all this new snow . . ." He didn't have to finish the sentence. They all knew that if the snow kept coming down the way it had been, they could be snowed in for the night.

Jenna turned her back on the window and abruptly crossed to the dining nook. Her group had been sent in to warm up and get a hot drink. She was exhausted, but even so she chafed against the delay. All she could think about was Jason, missing since daybreak. How cold he must be, and how tired . . . Grabbing a paper cup of mulled cider, she gulped it down without tasting it. Her hands shook as she crumpled the empty cup and forced it into the overflowing trash can.

It terrified her that some of the group was leaving while Jason was still out there.

She understood the arguments: that the other kids would be happier at home, that it was safer to take them down now, that clearing the cabins left more room for the adult rescuers . . . But seeing them all drive off in the bus felt too much like giving up. It made Jenna wonder who'd be leaving next.

And what would happen if they didn't find Jason before dark? Would everyone quit looking until morning? He couldn't possibly survive the night out there with no food, no water, no sleeping bag . . .

Jenna crossed her arms over her ribs and fought back tears. She'd been so looking forward to Christmas this year.

Now the thought of the coming morning filled her heart with dread.

Fourteen

Peter and Jesse stumbled frantically through the final distance to the summit of the knobby hill, the sky growing darker and the snow falling more thickly with every step they took.

"Jason!" Peter shouted, fighting to fill his lungs with the breath to do so.

"Jason!" Jesse screamed.

The snow deadened their voices as if they were shouting into barrels. They kept it up nevertheless, crisscrossing back and forth through the trees, covering the hilltop. "Jason! Jason!"

Nothing. The silence mocked them, expanding inside them until it was almost as big as their fear. The hilltop was as deserted as the place their hope had been. They stared at each other, too shattered to speak. Then Jesse whirled away.

"I was an idiot to bring us here!" he raged, kicking viciously at a snowdrift. Below them the back side of the hill fell steeply to the distant trees through a foreground peppered with boulders. "He couldn't have gotten this far! We should have

179

stayed in the search zone, where we might have done some good. Come on, let's go back."

But in the quiet following Jesse's explosion, Peter felt a strange calm. Whereas before he'd barely been able to pray, suddenly God felt very close. An odd stillness filled him, matching the stillness all around.

And then he heard a voice . . . so faint it was barely a whisper.

"Peter! Jesse! Help!"

Peter stiffened. "Did you hear that?"

"Peter! Help me!" Jason cried.

Jesse's head jerked up. He ran down over the edge of the hill and peered into the gathering darkness. Peter stayed where he was, trusting in the stillness and focusing his senses.

"There!" he shouted, pointing. Halfway down the rocky wrong side of the hill, barely a speck through the falling snow, he'd made out Jason's red parka.

"I see him!" Jesse hollered.

And then they were both charging down the slope toward Jason, barely noticing the hidden boulders that barked their shins or the fresh powder that filled their clothing. Jason was alive!

Jesse reached him first and scooped him up into his arms. "You scared us to death!" he cried, his voice crazy with joy and relief.

"Are you all right?" Peter asked, grabbing Jason from Jesse. Jason was well bundled up, still wearing his gloves and hat, but he was shivering uncontrollably and his teeth were chattering. "Are you hurt?"

"No," the boy got out.

Peter snatched off Jason's gloves to check his fingers for frostbite. They were icy cold but otherwise seemed all right. "How about your feet? Do your feet hurt?"

Jason shook his head. "No. My ankle, a little. I'm okay."

But when he looked into Peter's eyes, his face told a different story. First his lip began to quiver, then his chin. In the end he broke down completely.

"Oh, Peter," he sobbed. "I—I—"

"What is it, Jason?" Peter urged fearfully, nearly holding his breath for the answer. "What is it? You have to tell me."

"Peter, I lost the sled!"

"Wh—What?"

"I didn't mean to. I fell off and—"

"Are you kidding me?" Peter burst out laughing in his relief. "Jason, I don't care! I'm just so glad you're okay."

"But it was everyone's," Jason blubbered. "It was everyone's and I lost it."

"Forget about the stupid sled," Jesse told him,

181

echoing Peter's laughter. "I'll buy you guys another one—an even *better* one."

"I just . . . wanted to be big." Jason gulped his sobs into sniffles and wiped his red nose on his sleeve. "You don't know what it's like, being little all the time."

"Maybe I do," Peter said, patting his back. "It's tough having grown-ups make all the decisions about what's going to happen to you."

Jason nodded, and the motion sent fresh tears spilling down his cheeks. "Especially when they don't even ask you."

Peter didn't know what to say, so he just hugged the crying boy closer until Jesse reached for him again. Lifting Jason easily overhead, Jesse settled him on his shoulders.

"That's pretty big for now, isn't it?" he asked with surprising compassion. "Come on, bud. Let's go home."

"What's that noise?" Leah asked, turning and squinting eagerly into the darkening woods. "Did you hear something?"

Miguel hurried to her side and looked in the direction she pointed.

"I would have sworn . . . ," she said. "Oh, there they are! Look! Look!"

Peter and Jesse had just crested the nearest ridge—and Jason was riding on Jesse's shoulders!

"He's okay!" Peter shouted, breaking into a tired jog. "Tell the others. Tell everybody!"

Miguel ran forward to meet them. "Let me help you," he said, reaching to take the boy from Jesse.

But despite his obvious exhaustion, Jesse held Jason's shins tight. "No. I've got him," he said, never breaking stride. "Go get the rangers."

Leah hesitated only a second longer, then abandoned the guys to run off toward the trail as fast as she could, her long legs powering her through the drifts. Compared to Peter and Jesse, she and Miguel were still full of energy. She barely felt the effort as she pushed herself harder and harder to reach the mobile base, where the head ranger was directing the search operations.

"They found him! He's safe!" she cried, breaking through the trees. She waved her arms overhead. "Jason's safe!"

Cheers broke out from the small group crowding around the folding table full of maps, flashlights, radios, and other paraphernalia, and a rescue dog started barking somewhere. Leah ran the final distance and pulled up panting before the head ranger.

"Jesse and Peter . . . found him and . . . they're taking him back . . . to the cabins."

The ranger got on his radio, issuing a frenzy of orders that Leah barely heard. Air horns went off a moment later, three long blasts indicating that Jason had been found. Then everyone already on the trail started running toward the cabins, and Leah started running too. There was just enough light to see by as she pounded down the packed snow of the long trail.

A wicked cramp tormented her side and she had to slow to a walk before the cabins finally came into view, their lamps blazing brightly through the gloom. The front door of the nearer one stood open, spilling a wedge of yellow light onto the snow that illuminated the snowflakes floating through it. Just as Leah reached the level ground in front, a ranger rushed out. Jason lay bundled in blankets in his arms, a tuft of white-blond hair barely peeking from the dark green wool. Peter and Mrs. Brown followed the ranger to his truck. The four of them squeezed into the vehicle and drove away, the headlights sweeping the snowy road.

Jesse, Miguel, Jenna, Ben, Nicole, and Melanie came out to wave good-bye, having all beaten Leah down the trail.

"Where are they taking him?" Leah gasped to Jesse. "You said he was okay!"

"He is. They just want to take him to the hospital to make sure."

"They already checked his feet and everything," Jenna added. "He twisted one of his ankles a little, but there's not a hint of frostbite."

"He'll be fine," Jesse said firmly, as though using just the right tone would make it so.

"What a relief," said Melanie. "I was so afraid."

"Me too," Nicole admitted.

Miguel came to Leah's side to put an arm around her. "Are you cold?"

Leah shook her head. "But where was he? How did you guys find him?"

"It was exactly like I thought." A familiar hint of boastfulness crept into Jesse's voice. "After a few runs on the first hill, he decided to try for something bigger. You wouldn't believe how far he dragged that sled! Anyway, when he finally got to the hill he wanted, he was tired, and it was snowing pretty hard. But he decided to go down it anyway, and down the *back* side, which is even steeper than the front. That kid has guts."

He paused to smile proudly, and Jenna rushed in to pick up the tale Jason had apparently told in the cabin. "He fell off on the first run, though, and the sled kept going—"

"So he walked down the hill trying to find it," Ben piped up. "But by then it was snowing hard, and he didn't see where it went."

"The longer he looked, the more disoriented he got," Jesse continued. "He started getting scared, and then he twisted his ankle. He could walk, though, so he decided to go back to the top of the mountain to see if he could find his way from there—"

"Except that he found a cave!" Ben interrupted again.

185

Jesse shot Ben an annoyed glance for stealing his thunder. "Yeah. Halfway up he decided to rest by some rocks and found the entrance to a cave. He fell asleep in there, and when he woke up he was so cold and his ankle was so sore that he didn't want to leave. He stayed inside until he heard me and Peter calling."

Miguel squeezed Leah's shoulders tighter and turned to Jesse. "What a miracle. If you hadn't shown up and made Peter listen to you, we never would have found him today. And if we hadn't . . ."

Jesse looked shaken. But he didn't disagree.

Then Melanie tugged at Jesse's sleeve. "I have to go," she said in a low voice. "My dad's driving me home."

"Yeah, me too," Nicole said quickly, obviously relieved someone else had brought it up. "Merry Christmas, you guys."

"Merry Christmas," they all echoed.

"Call me tomorrow and let me know how Jason's doing," Leah said to Jenna.

"I will," Jenna promised.

Leah smiled mysteriously. "I might have something to tell you, too."

"We're home, Jenna," Caitlin whispered, shaking her gently awake.

Jenna reluctantly opened her eyes to find that

Mr. Conrad had already pulled their station wagon into the garage. Mary Beth was climbing out of the passenger seat, her auburn curls bright in the overhead light. The Conrads had ended up on different search teams, so Jenna had planned to catch up with Mary Beth on the drive home from the cabins, but five minutes into the conversation the blast from the car heater and the reassuring hum of the engine had put her fast asleep. All she'd managed to learn was that Mary Beth had worked with David Altmann, and that the expensive new gloves she'd acquired for her ski trip weren't anywhere near worth the money.

Mrs. Conrad appeared at the door between the house and garage just as Jenna emerged from the car. "You're back! Peter called and said Jason's fine, and his ankle isn't even sprained. Oh, Jenna, you look exhausted. Why don't you take a nice bubble bath and a nap before church? We'll take care of unpacking this stuff tomorrow."

"I can't," Jenna said, still holding on to the car door. Her legs felt as stiff as tree trunks, if tree trunks could have aching feet. "I have to go to the mall."

"To the mall?" Mary Beth exclaimed, laughing. "What have you been dreaming back there? It's Christmas Eve. The stores are closed by now."

Mary Beth was right. Tears welled up in her eyes. *The most important thing is that Jason's okay*, she reminded herself. *I'll find Peter something good on the twenty-sixth.*

But it wouldn't be the same. Even as she tried to reassure herself that Christmas wasn't about presents, she knew it would break her heart if Peter thought she didn't care enough about him to plan ahead.

Especially since he bought something for me two weeks ago. The tears overflowed her lashes, running down tracks that were starting to feel etched into her cheeks. Before she could wipe them away, her mother crossed the garage and wrapped her in a hug.

"Oh, sweetie, you're tired. Come inside and sit down."

The next thing Jenna knew, she was being led over the threshold into a house warm with the smells of a holiday dinner.

"You'll feel better when you've eaten," Mrs. Conrad said. "You can bathe after dinner and rest before church."

"I don't think I can sing tonight. I've been shouting myself hoarse all day."

Her mom nodded sympathetically. "Then we'll have to make do without you this year. Come into the kitchen and I'll make you some tea with honey."

But Jenna hesitated just inside the door. Once she went into the house, her younger sisters—Allison, Sarah, and especially Maggie—would have a hundred questions each about the search and Jason's eventual rescue. Then there would be dinner. And catching up with Mary Beth. And a bath. And a dozen little things to do before church. Once she got mixed up in all that, she'd never get the chance to sneak back out. And that meant definitely no present for Peter.

"Do you think every single store is closed?" she blurted out unhappily. "I mean, maybe one of the department stores . . . or something at the mall . . ."

Her mother stopped trying to herd her inside, a concerned frown on her face. "What was it you wanted to buy?"

"Just . . . something for Peter. I ruined that shirt I was making, so I was going to buy him a sweater."

"Did you have one picked out?"

Jenna shook her head miserably. "I didn't even like the idea that much, but I knew I'd only have a couple of hours to shop when we got home. And now . . ." Her throat was so constricted she couldn't continue.

Her mom gave her shoulders a sympathetic squeeze. "You've had a tough enough day already without upsetting yourself about this. Besides, I have an idea I think you might like."

Motioning Jenna into the den, Mrs. Conrad began rummaging through a pile of shopping bags in a corner of the room. Jenna sank deeply into the sofa cushions, too exhausted even to guess what her mother was looking for.

"I actually bought this for you, but we can always get you another one," Mrs. Conrad said, her back to her daughter. "Ah, here it is."

She spun around with something shiny in her hands. "Ta-da! What do you think of this?"

Fifteen

"Aren't you going to say anything?" Melanie demanded, unable to hold back any longer.

Mr. Andrews shrugged as he closed the refrigerator door, a bottle of beer in his hand. "What do you want me to say?"

She didn't know. She wasn't even sure it mattered, so long as he said *something*. All the way home, on the long, dark drive from the cabins at Rabbit Ridge, she'd been expecting some sort of lecture. Waiting for one, actually. But now that they were home, and it was clear no lecture was forthcoming, Melanie didn't feel relieved.

She felt cheated.

Any normal parent would demand to know why I took off on Christmas Eve to drive to Iowa without permission, she thought sullenly. But instead of insisting on explanations, her father had simply parked the sports car in the garage, entered the house through the connecting door, and gone directly to the refrigerator, leaving Melanie to follow or not, as she liked. Obviously he was finished with her for the evening. Well, she wasn't finished with him.

"You ought to have plenty to say!" she exploded. "How come you can search for some stranger's kid in the middle of a snowstorm but you can't even talk to me?"

He twisted the cap off his beer. "I didn't think—"

"You never think! And could we have just one conversation without you drinking all the way through it?"

He put the open beer down on the counter, but Melanie had had enough. She lunged toward it, all the bitterness she'd held back over the last two years rushing to the surface as she grabbed the slippery bottle and flipped it upside down over the sink.

"I'm sick of this!" she told him, jerking the bottle up and down to try to empty it faster. It slipped from her hand and crashed into the sink.

"What are you doing?" he began, stepping toward her.

"I want you to stop it!" she screamed. "Are you planning to drink yourself to death?"

"Come on, Melanie. I'm not that bad."

"You are! You are that bad and you don't even know it! Am I going to be visiting some headstone instead of you next year too?"

He raised one eyebrow, trying for humor. "Are you planning to do this again next year?"

"You know what I mean!"

"No, Mel, I really don't."

"I don't want you to drink anymore. I don't want you to lie around the house in your bathrobe all day. I don't want to watch you sulk about Mom from now until you die. I want a normal life."

Mr. Andrews shook his head. "There's nothing normal about—"

"As normal as we can make it, then! Mom's dead, Dad. And we have to let her go." The harshness of her words surprised her, but even as they tumbled out she knew she was right. "You owe me that, at least."

He closed his eyes. "I can't let her go, Mel. I keep thinking there's something I could have done differently. I could have made her drive a safer car, or I could have driven her myself—"

"It was an *accident*, Dad."

"Not to me." He backed up to the kitchen counter until his hands gripped the edge, flexing unconsciously. "I'll always feel like it was my fault."

"Why does it have to be anyone's fault? Why can't it just have happened?"

"Because it *didn't* just happen—it happened to me!"

"It happened to us, Dad. Do you want me to give up too? Do you want me to start skipping school and drinking every day?"

Mr. Andrews's eyes opened wider. "You'd better not."

193

"Then you'd better give me a reason not to! Because it would be easy, Dad. Giving up is so easy."

Her father observed her carefully, as if to gauge her seriousness. "That's blackmail."

She tried to shrug, wanting desperately to make him think she was calm and in control of the situation. But she didn't have it in her to act as if she didn't care. The tears started to flow despite her efforts to hold them back.

"All I'm saying is, if you're going down, I'm going down with you," she managed to choke out somehow. "I've had enough of this."

"Aw, Mel."

He moved to put his arms around her. It was her chance to tell him everything in her heart, the things she most wanted and feared, but all she could do was cry. And after a while his breathing changed, and she knew he was crying too.

"I'm sorry," he murmured. "I'm so sorry. Mel. I swear."

She lifted her tear-streaked face hopefully. "So you're going to stop drinking, then?"

He winced and shook his head. "You don't even know what you're asking for. It doesn't work that way."

"Maybe I know more than you think."

Her past mistakes suddenly hung in the air between them, waiting to be revealed, and in the same instant Melanie realized she was prepared to say

194

whatever it took to get his attention. Anything. And there was so much to choose from . . .

Mr. Andrews seemed to sense the presence of stories he didn't want to hear. Or maybe he knew he'd lost the right to ask. He searched her eyes a long, long time, and then he closed his own.

"I . . . I'll think about it," he said, taking a deep breath. "Maybe I'll make some calls on Monday."

She smiled through her tears and hugged him tighter.

"You know it's not that easy," he warned. "I'm only saying I'll try."

"And that's the only Christmas present I want this year," she told him, squeezing with all her strength. "That's it."

He returned her embrace, then broke into a rueful chuckle. "Way to think small," he said.

They made hot chocolate to replace his beer and sipped it at the breakfast bar, gazing out at their backyard. There were no Christmas lights, but the gardener had replaced the white plastic covers on their landscaping lamps with red and green ones. The lights spilled festive, stained-glass shadows across the unmarked snow. It actually felt a little like Christmas as Melanie said good-night to her father and headed up to bed.

Except that the tree was gone from the living room. She noted its absence as she walked by on her way to the stairs. *Dad must have tossed it already,* she thought, and she was almost sorry now. Sorry they hadn't decorated it, sorry she hadn't given it a chance, sorry he hadn't asked if she wanted it first . . .

Well, what do you expect, taking off on Christmas Eve? How was he supposed to know you'd change your mind?

She shrugged as she climbed the stairs. She wasn't going to worry about it now. After the day she'd had, all she wanted to do was take a hot shower, climb into bed, and bury herself under soft down and pink flannel. She turned the last corner on the landing and headed toward her open bedroom door.

A strange glow filled her doorway, seeping into the hall. Melanie hurried a little, wondering what she could have left turned on. But when she stepped into her bedroom, the answer was the very last thing she'd expected. Her hand flew to her mouth, and tears rushed to her eyes again.

Her father hadn't taken the tree outside. He'd carried it up to her bedroom and decorated it with every tiny colored light and every ornament they owned. The fir sat regally in a corner, its twinkling branches sheltering a pile of brightly wrapped presents. Melanie crept slowly across her snow white carpet and buried her face in its fragrant needles.

Can this really be what it seems? she wondered, hoping so with all her heart. *Is this a new beginning?*

* * *

Peter opened the small flannel pouch slowly, enjoying the suspense of wondering what was in it. Jenna sat beside him in the otherwise deserted Sunday-school classroom, twisting her hands nervously.

"I hope you like it," she said for the second time. "There was a little problem."

Reaching inside, he drew out a hinged double picture frame of gleaming sterling silver. The frame was closed, and he opened it quickly, excited. Inside were spaces for two snapshot-sized pictures, and on the left was a sight that made Peter smile: a photo of himself and Jenna in sixth grade, mugging for the camera in her backyard tree house. On the right, a light blue slip of paper had been inserted in place of a second photograph. Jenna's best handwriting looped across it in pink ink:

From 6th grade to 11th and still going strong! Save this place for a happy face— my dad will take our picture together tomorrow.

Peter smiled happily, but before he could say how much he liked her gift, Jenna burst into a long explanation.

"I tried to make you a shirt," she said apologetically. "I was almost done with it when I made a mis-take and cut a hole in the middle of the back." She gestured to the blue-and-tan flannel pouch the picture frame had come in. "I made that with a scrap, so at least you know what it would have looked like. Then I decided to buy you a ski sweater, but between going to winter camp and Jason getting lost and—"

"Jenna, stop worrying. This is great!"

"It is?"

"Of course! A good picture of you is the one thing I really wanted." He laughed as he pointed to the sixth-grade shot. "I don't even remember posing for this. Why didn't you ever show it to me before?"

"My mom found it while we were away. I guess it got stuck in a drawer somewhere."

"It sure brings back some memories."

Then suddenly he remembered he hadn't given Jenna his gift yet. Putting the frame back into its pouch, he grabbed the coat he'd thrown across the table in front of them. In its right side pocket, he found what he was looking for: a small, red-wrapped package with a gold star bow. He handed it to her eagerly. "The second I saw this I thought . . . well, uh . . . I just hope you like it."

"What is it?" Jenna asked, bringing it up to her ear as if she expected to hear something ticking.

She shook the box back and forth, then listened again. "Is it breakable?"

"I hope not," said Peter, laughing. "If it is, you just took care of it."

Jenna looked alarmed as she ripped off the wrapping paper. Inside a shiny green box, the silver dove pin nestled on a bed of white cotton.

"Peter!" she gasped, snatching the pin from the box and holding it up to the light. "I love it."

Her hands shook slightly as she removed the round little back from the tie-tack–style pin and held the dove to the stand-up collar of her dress, trying to pierce the crisp white fabric.

"Here. Let me help you." With his left hand he held her collar taut, pushing the pin through it easily with his right. He didn't fumble a bit until she handed him the back of the pin to finish the job. Then he had to reach slightly inside her high collar, where he couldn't see what he was doing.

"Peter, you're tickling," she protested, giggling.

"Stop squirming if you don't want a hole right through your jugular," he said, as if he hadn't noticed how soft and warm the skin that pressed the backs of his fingers was. "There. That's on now, I think."

He let go and she double-checked it with her fingertips. "Feels all right to me. How does it look?"

He wanted to tell her how beautiful she was,

with or without the pin, but he couldn't think of a way to say it that didn't sound stupid. "I think it looks real nice. And when you put on your choir robe, everyone will still be able to see it up there."

Jenna smiled. "Decoration will be my primary contribution anyway, since I'll be mouthing half the words." She put a hand to her sore throat. "I probably should have sat out, but it's Christmas Eve, you know? Besides, the pressure's completely off because Liz Farley is singing my solos. My mom already called her."

Peter smiled. "The pressure's off of you, you mean. I'll bet Liz is a little nervous."

Jenna laughed and shook her head. "No, she's completely thrilled. I ought to be hoarse more often."

"Well, it's a small price to pay for finding Jason safe. There was a point out there today when I'd have volunteered to be hoarse for the rest of my life in exchange for a decent clue."

"That's because you can't sing," Jenna teased, a twinkle in her eyes.

"Very funny. And you know what the funniest part is? Jason's in bed right now, sawing some serious logs, and we're already back to our normal lives like nothing ever happened."

"Well, *almost* like nothing happened. I imagine I'll saw some pretty big logs tonight myself."

Peter nodded. "I had a nap before I picked you up," he confided.

"So did I!"

A noise in the courtyard outside made Peter glance at his watch. "If you're going to lip-sync, you'd better go put on your choir robe," he said reluctantly.

"I will in a minute. You know what, Peter? I think this is going to be the very best Christmas ever."

"How so?"

"Well, we got off to a scary start, but Jason is fine, and the Junior Explorers love their new bus. Mary Beth is home . . . David's home . . . Eight Prime's still together . . ." She paused shyly. "*We're* together."

Peter's heart jumped at the unexpected words. A second later it began to race.

Jenna was leaning toward him, bringing her face close to his. She hesitated, then leaned a little closer. Peter froze, afraid that one false move might shatter the moment. For a second everything seemed to have stopped. He could smell the shampoo she'd used that evening and count each one of her eyelashes. He heard his heart thumping and wondered if she heard it too. Then Jenna leaned over the last two inches and kissed him lightly on the lips.

"Merry Christmas, Peter," she murmured.

Peter felt as if he were floating an inch or two off his chair. "Merry Christmas," he replied happily.

Jenna had been wrong when she'd said this was *going* to be the best Christmas ever. As far as he was concerned, it already was.

The next to the last song in the midnight service was "Angels We Have Heard on High." Jenna had thought she wouldn't be able to hit a single high note, but she'd found that her voice had been gaining strength all night. As the hymn came to a chorus of glorias near the end, she found her full voice for a moment and sang out with all her heart.

Everyone in the choir was singing with equal passion. They had never sounded better, and Jenna knew that their inspiration came both from the joy of the event they sang about and from the true spirit of warmth and friendship that filled the church that night. Their voices were lifted as high as their hearts.

Jenna smiled down at her mother, who was leading the choir, before her eyes darted to her father and all five sisters in the jam-packed pews. The Conrads had places beside the Altmanns, with David sitting next to Mary Beth. Jenna's eyes met Peter's, and her hand reached up to touch the dove pin shining from her collar. He smiled in return and patted the pocket of his jacket, where he'd put her picture frame.

And then the choir paused to ready for the final song. The lights dimmed. Reverend Thompson stood and lit a single white taper. The flame flickered, then held, as the first strains of music filled the church again:

Silent night, holy night. All is calm, all is bright.

The congregation rose to its feet, each member holding a candle. The minister moved to the front pew and with his flame lit new ones on either side of the aisle. Soon everyone was crowding candles around the nearest burning wick, until there were dozens alight, being used to light dozens more. The flame passed from person to person, spreading until it reached back to the very last pew and out to the farthest corners. The entire church was illuminated with the soft golden glow of candles.

Jenna looked down from the choir, thinking she'd never seen anything prettier. She was so tired and so happy she barely knew whether to laugh or to cry.

In the end the tears won out, blurring the perfect scene in front of her into something even more beautiful.

Sixteen

"Here, Heather, this one's for you." Nicole felt extremely unselfish and mature as she handed her sister another present to open, but the fact was that she had used the excuse of reaching for it to scope out who the really big box behind the tree was for. The tag said NICOLE.

What can it be? she wondered excitedly as she feigned interest in the gift Heather was opening—a sweater or pajamas by the feel of it.

The Brewster tradition was that presents were opened after Christmas breakfast, and always one at a time. Nicole's unmarried aunt Sophie always joined them, although Nicole didn't understand why; she hardly got anything compared to the rest of them. Then, in the afternoon, they'd go to her grandparents' house for dinner and repeat the entire process.

"Oh, cool!" Heather cried, holding up a lime green Teen Extreme sweatshirt. "Look, Nicole!"

"They had sweatshirts?" Nicole heard herself say

204

weakly, all the while praying there wasn't a similar box with her name on it somewhere in the mountain of presents surrounding the tree. She'd never wear it. Forget about the color, which was frightening enough—what would people think?

Heather peeled off her bathrobe and pulled the sweatshirt on over the top of her nightgown. Jumping to her feet, she turned in a little circle so everyone could see her putrid green shirt, striped red flannel skirt, and fluffy pink slippers. "How do I look?"

"Goofy," Nicole said automatically. It felt strange to see the Teen Extreme logo there in their living room—and what was even stranger was that the sight gave her a pang. Not that she missed the class. No way. But it hadn't been *entirely* horrible either.

She sighed. If one of those ugly sweatshirts turned up with her name on it, she supposed she could wear it around the house, if it would spare her parents' feelings.

"Be nice to your sister," Mrs. Brewster said, her tone on autopilot. She pointed from where she sat on the living room sofa. "And hand that red box to your father."

Aunt Sophie got out of her chair. "I'm going to make some more tea. Can I bring something for anyone else?"

"More cookies," Heather said immediately.

"No more cookies," Mrs. Brewster said sharply.

Nicole's father was opening his present when the telephone rang, startling everyone.

"Sophie will get it," said Mrs. Brewster. "She's already in the kitchen."

A moment later Aunt Sophie came out with a fresh cup of tea—and a big plate of cookies. "The phone's for you, Nicole. Leah somebody."

"Leah?" Nicole repeated, scrambling to her feet.

"Why is she calling you now?" her mother said irritably. "We're right in the middle of presents. Tell her you'll call her back later."

"All right," Nicole agreed, her mind on that big box behind the tree. She hurried into the kitchen, planning to keep the call short. "Hello?"

"Am I interrupting something?" Leah asked anxiously. "Or do you have a minute to talk?"

"Well . . . I'm a little busy, but I can talk for a minute. We're opening our presents and my mom has a fit if everyone isn't watching."

"Nicole!" her father called from the living room.

"Make that *half* a minute," Nicole amended.

"I won't keep you long. I just wanted to give you my Christmas present."

"What?" No one in Eight Prime had mentioned anything to Nicole about exchanging gifts. Were they all supposed to get each other something? Her quilted robe seemed suddenly too warm, her hand slick on the plastic receiver.

"You didn't have to get me anything, Leah," she said, knowing she couldn't reciprocate.

Leah chuckled. "I know, and I hadn't planned to. But something's come up and, well . . . how'd you like to go to California with me next month?"

For a moment no words would come. Nicole's knuckles turned white on the telephone, and her blood made such a roar in her ears that she couldn't even hear her family's impatient chatter. Then all the words spilled out at once.

"To the U.S. Girls contest?" she shrieked. "You're inviting *me*? Oh, wow! Oh, Leah! *Yes!* I can't believe you picked *me*! Of course, I did kind of help you win in the first place. I mean, if it wasn't for me you never would have entered. But—"

"Hold your horses," Leah broke in, laughing. "I've invited Melanie and Jenna, too. I'm hoping we can all go together."

"Your parents aren't going?" Nicole asked, stunned.

"They have something they need to do here. But the whole event is chaperoned like crazy, and it's not as if we're babies. Melanie said she can definitely go, and Jenna thinks she'll get permission too, once her parents check it out. So I'm hoping yours will—"

"Oh, they will!" Nicole said hurriedly. She wouldn't take no for an answer on something as important as this. Besides, they owed her for that

Teen Extreme thing. They owed her big. "I'm going. Count me in."

"Good. I think it'll be pretty fun. I hope it will anyway."

"Are you kidding? This is going to be great! The best! Wait until everyone at school finds out. They're going to be sick that the four of us are going to Hollywood—and in January! We'll be like celebrities."

But Nicole had no sooner hung up the phone than she realized there was at least one person who wasn't likely to congratulate her on her good fortune.

Uh-oh, she thought, feeling slightly queasy. *Courtney isn't going to like this one little bit.*

After all, Courtney had sat through the endless preliminary contest where Leah had won the Missouri title. Courtney had even suggested that four girls should go to the California finals: namely, Leah, Melanie, Nicole, and *Courtney.* Nicole didn't want to hear what her best friend would say when she found out Jenna had been invited instead of her. The taunts about the God Squad would never end.

Unless she doesn't speak to me at all, Nicole thought unhappily. *And that's probably more likely.*

"What's this?" Melanie said, bending to pick up an open cardboard box on her front doorstep.

Under a thick, protective layer of shredded paper, she found a second box, this one decorated in gold foil and white ribbon. A white star-shaped tag bore only two words: FOR MELANIE.

The sun was shining in a clear blue sky, reflecting dazzlingly off a layer of fresh, clean snow, but Melanie barely noticed how beautiful the weather was in her curiosity over the box.

"What could it be?" she muttered. "And from who?"

There was nothing on either the box or the tag to give her any clue. Completely forgetting she'd been on her way to find a spot for her new bird feeder, she took the box back into the entryway and closed the door behind her.

Inside, sunshine poured through the windows, bleaching the cool gray marble and concrete to shades much closer to white. Her mother's paintings were alive in the slanting beams, splashing color across every wall. Blind to this scene too, Melanie sat down on the floor, impatient to solve the mystery.

"What are you doing?" her father asked, wandering out from the kitchen with a cup of coffee in his hand. "I thought you were picking a spot for me to hang that feeder."

"I am. In a minute."

The gold foil wrapping paper came off in one piece. Melanie popped the tape that held the lid closed and pawed through more shredded paper inside until her fingertips touched something pointy, something delicate. Carefully she pulled a handful of packing out. Only then did she know who the gift was from.

"Jesse," she whispered, amazed.

Inside the box was a porcelain angel, shockingly similar to the one she had left at her mother's grave. Only this one was larger and much more elaborately made. She lifted the sculpture into the sunlight, wondering when he'd found time to buy it.

The angel's iridescent wings spread high, translucent at their edges. Her golden hair spilled to her heels, at the same time giving the illusion of moving with a breeze. A long white gown reached to her bare feet. The only major difference between the figurine and the ornament was that the ornament had carried a paintbrush, whereas this sculpted angel's hands were open, palm up, her arms arranged as if she were dancing.

"Nice," her father said. "I think somebody likes you," he added before he went back to the kitchen.

A small folded slip of paper had been taped to the sculpture's base. Melanie removed it and read the message inside:

Not half as beautiful as you are. J

She didn't even know what to think. Should she be mad at him for spying on her? Because he had to have spied on her somehow, to know what the angel she'd brought to her mother looked like. Or should she be touched? She wouldn't have believed that Jesse could be so sweet, so thoughtful. . . .

Melanie gazed at the delicate porcelain in her hands and felt herself choking up. *No. Stop it.*

Just because she and Jesse had been forced to spend a day together and had shared a couple of nearly human moments . . . Just because he'd agreed to drive her all the way to Iowa without even knowing why, and had refused to accept gas money, and had been the shoulder she'd cried on when things got too weird . . .

He's still a flirt.

And she still didn't trust him. She read his note again.

Ha! He probably says that to all the girls, she scoffed. *At least at first.*

Although she couldn't quite imagine him saying it to Vanessa, and she didn't think he'd said it to Nicole either. *Besides, if he was just stringing me along, wouldn't he have gotten tired of it by now?*

She'd never admit it to him, but there probably wasn't a girl at school Jesse couldn't have if he put his mind to it. He had to know that. So why did he choose to be as lonely as he obviously was?

Better question: Why did she?

She turned the angel slowly in her hands. *Maybe I ought to give Jesse a chance.*

Find out what happens next in Clearwater Crossing #8, *One Real Thing*.

About the Author

Laura Peyton Roberts holds an M.A. in English from San Diego State University. A native Californian, she lives with her husband in San Diego.

Dear Reader,

Thanks for visiting Clearwater Crossing!

If you enjoyed this book, I hope you'll come back to check on the continuing adventures of Peter, Jenna, Jesse, Melanie, Leah, Miguel, Nicole, and Ben. Readers say they like these characters because they remind them of real people—people they know, or maybe even themselves. The characters don't always find life easy; they struggle with their families, friendships, and faith, and in the process make the same types of mistakes so many of us do. Ultimately, however, acceptance, perseverance, and a genuine desire to become better people lead them to happier times. Things in Clearwater Crossing don't always turn out the way the characters hope, but life is sometimes like that, isn't it?

If you've been following this series from the beginning, then by now you know how I love a good cliffhanger. Having a friend in suspense along with you can make waiting to see what happens next that much more exciting. So why not share Clearwater Crossing with a friend? How would the two of you handle some of the experiences our characters have had? My publisher has included a special blank page so that if you'd like to pass this installment of the series along, you can write a personal note to your friend first. And if you'd prefer to keep your copy, you can still use the page to share your enthusiasm with your friend.

Once again, thank you for choosing this book. I hope to see you back in Clearwater Crossing real soon!

Sincerely,

Laura Peyton Roberts